Star Child

First published 2008 by Kingfisher

This edition published by Macmillan Children's Books
a division of Macmillan Publishers Limited
20 New Wharf Road, London N1 9RR
Basingstoke and Oxford
Associated companies throughout the world
www.panmacmillan.com

ISBN 978-0-330-51032-5

Star Child

Zodiac Girls

Cathy Hopkins

MACMILLAN CHILDREN'S BOOKS

Chapter One

Zodiac Girl

Thebe's list of things to do

Look up this month's (May) horoscope on the
   computer.

Do homework.

Lay out clothes for school.

Do internet shop for groceries.

Leave list of things to do for Mrs Watson,
   housekeeper.

6) Practise ice-skating.

"Omigiddyaunt!" I said to our black cat, Cosmo,
who looked up with sleepy eyes from the end of my
bed. "This is *so* fantastic."

I was sitting at my desk and I went back to the
website I'd been looking at on my computer to double
check that I hadn't dreamt what I'd seen. Actually, it
was my dad's website: www.battyestars.org. Dad being
Benjamin Battye, the celebrity astrologer. He does a
weekly column for the *Sunday State* newspaper, a

1

monthly column in *Divine Divas*, the glossy designer mag, and he's on TV every Friday on Good Morning Britain talking about what's up and coming in the sky for the weekend and discussing a chosen celebrity's horoscope each month. I couldn't wait to share my news with him. I got up and raced to the top of the stairs.

"Dad. Da-*ad*!"

"What is it, munchkin?" Dad called, from somewhere on the ground floor.

"I think it's going to be me this month."

"I said it might be, didn't I? Come on down and we'll double check on my computer and see what's next."

I took a quick glance in the mirror at the end of the hall. A small thirteen year-old girl with brown eyes, coffee-coloured skin and braided hair looked back at me. "Today's going to be your day," I said to my reflection, then I took the stairs down two at a time and clomped along the wooden floor to find him. This was the best thing that could ever happen and it was happening to me. *Me*. Thebe Battye.

I'd just seen it written in my horoscope on the computer. Planetary line-ups like that only happen once in a lifetime and sometimes not at all for some people. I felt so happy, I felt like doing a cartwheel. Usually if anything exciting happened it was to someone else in my family. They're all so glam, swanning about living extraordinary lives, being the centre of attention, and I'm usually there in the background being Little Miss Boring to whom nothing ever happens.

My mum's famous too. She didn't used to be when we (me and my elder sister Pat) were younger. She was a stay-at-home mum then, but about five years ago she signed up to do a business degree at the Open University and discovered that she had a talent for making money. She lost three stone in weight, got herself some hair extensions so instead of her hair being short and frizzy, it was suddenly shoulder length and sleek and then she went out and bought a new wardrobe of clothes. It was a case of, "Watch out world, here comes Estella Battye, business woman supreme and a force to be reckoned with!"

Dad says it's because she is an Aries and Aries is ruled by the planet Mars which is the planet of war! It's true, Mum is not someone to mess with when she has a project on! Now she runs Battye Enterprises which deals with everything and anything to do with astrology. All aspects. You name it, she sources it then sells it: star-sign mugs, T-shirts, pendants, rings, books, cards, key rings, personalized horoscopes written by Dad. He had always been famous but Mum made him *rich* and famous. When she started raking in the mega bucks, she bought us a bigger house and named it Zodiac Lodge. It's near Osbury, which is a village built on a sacred site. Legend has it that it was a home of the ancient gods and twinned with Mount Olympus in Greece. All the rooms are decorated on an astrological theme. For example, the bathroom is the Pisces room as that's the sign of the fish as well as being a water sign, and Pisces is ruled by the planet Neptune and Neptune is known as the King of the sea – so the bathroom has a strong marine theme. It's blue and green in there with pictures of fish and mermaids and a border around the top with shells on it. Very pretty. The décor of the whole house was worked out that way – each room with its own theme according to the stars. My best friend, Rachel, loves coming here and looking into all the rooms. She says it's like visiting a colourful art gallery.

I almost collided with Pat who came out of the kitchen holding a glass of juice. "Woah, slow down. What's the hurry?" she said.

"Me. I think I'm Zodiac Girl this month. Isn't that fantastic?"

Pat shrugged. "If you say so," she said and sauntered on. Pat isn't interested in astrology at all. Mum and Dad named her Mahina when she was born. She was born under the sign of Cancer and Cancerians are ruled by the Moon. Mahina means the moon and I think it's a lovely, romantic name. Not my sister though. When she was nine she demanded that no one call her that any more and she changed her name to Pat. *Pat!* She doesn't look like a Pat. She looks like a Mahina. She's very pretty with big brown eyes, a heart-shaped face and black hair (extensions, like Mum) half way down her back.

Her room on the top floor is the only one that doesn't have a Zodiac theme – at least not any more. It was decorated to reflect the Moon and had a navy ceiling covered in teeny fairy lights that twinkled like stars. Sleeping in there was like being outside on a cloudless night, plus there is a skylight in there so part of what you were looking at was the real sky. When Pat was ten, she chucked out all the star posters and the Moon-shaped lamp and painted the room white, even the ceiling. On her door, she put a poster saying KEEP OUT ON PAIN OF DEATH. STRICTLY NO ZODIAC STUFF IN HERE. ALSO ON PAIN OF DEATH. And then she added a skull and crossbones to emphasize that she was serious. Dad says she reacts like that because she has the Moon in Scorpio and being cynical about things like horoscopes is typical of someone with a birth chart like hers. She's one of the most popular girls in our school. She's sixteen and there's a long line of boys queuing up for her attention. She usually breaks their hearts though, simply because she can.

I found Dad stretched out in his study at the back of the house. Dad liked to dress as if he was still in the Caribbean (which is where our family is originally from, although Pat and I were born in England.) He was wearing one of his brightly-coloured patterned shirts with red parrots on it, long shorts and sandals. With his shoulder-length dreadlocks, he looked like a reggae musician. Mum and he do look funny together, like she's Mrs Straight and he's Mr Chilled Out.

The study is the room that has been themed around the planet Mercury which is the planet of communication. Also Mercury was known in the time of the Greek gods as the winged messenger. Mercury is the ruling planet for both Gemini and Virgo. Dad is Gemini and I am a Virgo so we have the Mercury connection in common. Dad thought it was appropriate to have his study as the Mercury room as that's where he does all his communicating – through his computer, his phone and all his books are in there. Loads of them. Some of them are ancient with worn, leather covers with faded paper inside and the words are written in beautiful handwriting. It's a large, cool room with high ceilings and French windows that open out onto the back when the weather's warm. Dad has two old leather sofas in front of a marble fireplace where he likes to lie out and read. He sometimes reads five or six books at a time and he leaves them open all over the place so I often trip over them. On the walls are some paintings he got in India and they depict the various planets in astrology. In the corner near the desk, he has a life-size bronze statue of Mercury which one of his Hollywood clients bought him as a thank you. I personally think it's a bit rude as the statue is in the nudie pants, and sometimes when you sit on the sofa, its dangly bits are exactly at eye level. Not particularly what I want to be looking at when I'm in there having a cup of tea and a crumpet with Dad, thank you very much. I put a yellow sticky note on it once to cover up the "not-so-private" private parts. Dad thought it was hysterically funny and called the whole family in to look. I had never been so embarrassed in my whole life. I find it annoying being in Dad's study sometimes because it's so untidy and I am dying to clear up, but he won't let me touch a thing.

"It's my room," he says. "And I have my own system." It's weird, Virgos and Geminis might both have the same ruling planet but as star signs go, they are sooooo different. Virgos like things neat.

"Here, take a look at this," said Dad, and he beckoned me over to his shelf where he heaved down one of his ancient books. When it thudded onto his desk, a cloud of dust blew up and made me sneeze.

"A-chOOOOOOO! Honestly Dad, one day I'm going to sneak in here with a feather duster and a face mask and give the place a good clean!"

"You dare. I like it like this. It's lived in."

"A-CHOOOOOOOOOOOOOOOO!" I sneezed again.

Dad ignored me and carried on turning pages. "Ah, here we are," he said. "I knew it was in here somewhere."

I glanced down at the page he had opened the book on. The words Zodiac Girls were written in large, old-fashioned letters and were illustrated in different coloured inks with a night sky behind them.

"Let's see what it says," said Dad and he leaned in to study the page closer. "Hmm, yes, yes, ruling planets, we know all about that. The planets are here in human form. Yes, yes…"

I had seen this chapter ages ago because I loved to go through Dad's books, especially the older ones. I liked the sense of history in them, the feeling that someone in some ancient time, before the days of spellcheck and copy and paste, had sat and written every word and even illustrated some of them. I remembered reading that there were such people as Zodiac Girls but I hadn't paid it too much attention until recently when Dad had said that he suspected that I might be one.

I leaned over his shoulder and read: "Zodiac Girls. Somewhere on the earth, every month, one maiden is chosen to be a Zodiac Girl. This entitles her to:

1) A gift of jewellery to wear that is appropriate to her star sign.

2) A means of communicating with the planets.

3) The assistance of the planets who are all here on earth in disguise as normal people.

4) The ruling planet of each sign will act as guardian for one month only."

Awesome, I thought as I glanced down at the list of star signs and their ruling planets.

Ruling planet	Star sign
Sun	Leo
Moon	Cancer
Mercury	Gemini and Virgo
Venus	Taurus and Libra
Mars	Aries
Jupiter	Sagittarius
Saturn	Capricorn
Uranus	Aquarius
Neptune	Pisces
Pluto	Scorpio

"You know the part about the planets being here in human form?" I asked.

"Yes."

"What will Mercury be here as?"

Dad looked at the book. "Hmm, Mercury, the

winged messenger. Well your guess is as good as mine." He flipped the page over. "See, this book is centuries old so how he appears may change from age to age. He would have been something to do with messages and communication though I would imagine. How that manifests today, no doubt we'll find out." Dad pointed at a birth chart on the right-hand side of the page. "But look here. This is the chart of a typical Zodiac Girl showing how the planetary line-up will look when it's her month as Zodiac Girl."

I glanced down at the page and saw the birth chart on the page. To someone who didn't know, it would look like a circle with a smaller circle inside it and lines drawn across it. To me, though – I knew at a glance what most of it meant. I'd watched Dad work out birth charts for his clients just about every day of my life. I'd never known a home that lived and breathed astrology so much. Like, most babies had cot mobiles with ducks or teddy bears or fish on them, I had had a mobile with the ten planets hanging from it. By the time I was five, I knew the stars as well as I knew my alphabet. I also knew that there was more to astrology than the horoscopes in magazines or newspapers. I knew that each and every person's horoscope was different, depending on what time they were born and where they were born and where the planets were in the sky in relation to that. It was a real science, not hocus pocus as some of Dad's critics claimed.

"Now, quick," said Dad, "print out the planetary line for your chart for this month. I've got it up on the screen now."

I went over to the computer, pressed print and a second later the sheet of paper was in my hand. I took it over to Dad who placed it on the left-hand side of the page of the book. We looked at the chart in the book and then at mine.

"Bingo," said Dad.

"Bingo," I replied.

They matched each other perfectly. Same line up.

Just at that moment, there was a knock at the front door. We heard Pat go to open it then a moment later there was the muffled sound of voices. Soon after, there were footsteps in the corridor and Pat opened the study door. She looked bright-eyed and flushed. "Er Thebe. Someone here for you."

"Who is it?"

"Some motorbike messenger," she said then she lowered her voice and whispered, "and he's a *total* babe, like a Greek god in biker leathers."

A tingle of excitement went through me. I smiled at Dad and he winked back at me. "Oh, I think we might know exactly who it is," I said. "Erm… tell him to come in. We've been expecting him."

Chapter Two

Hermie

"Welcome," said Dad, doing an awkward type of bow-curtsey, as if he wasn't sure how to behave with a six-foot motorbike messenger in his study. The stranger appeared equally unsure and looked around at the paintings and books in amazement. He was just as Pat had described him, about eighteen, maybe older, but a total boy babe with a handsome face, a chiselled jaw and a tall, broad-shouldered body. He reminded me of the statues of the Greek and Roman gods that we'd seen in the British Museum when we went there on a school trip – too good looking to be true, and yet here he was standing in front of us radiating health and charisma. I had a feeling that I was staring at him open mouthed and I made a conscious effort to close my jaw. Not that he noticed. He had seen the statue of Mercury and was staring at it in surprise. It did resemble him and I wondered how he felt about finding a statue of himself with no clothes on in my Dad's study.

"It's Mercury," said Dad with a glance at the statue, "and I'm Benjamin Battye."

"And I'm Hermes, but you can call me Hermie," said the messenger boy.

"Isn't Hermes the Greek name for the god of travel and communication?" asked Dad with a sly wink at me, "and Mercury is the Roman name for the same god?"

Hermie looked impressed. "Hmm, you know your gods," he replied and then opened his jacket to reveal a T-shirt underneath with the words Mercury Communications written on it.

"And I know my planets," said Dad with another wink.

"Really?" asked Hermie.

Dad nodded, tapped his nose and indicated the paintings and posters on the wall and the books on his shelves. Hermie took a closer look at some of the titles while I desperately tried to think of something to say, but my brain seemed to have turned to mush and all I could do was stare.

Dad pointed at the ancient book that was still open on the chapter about Zodiac Girls. "See this Hermie?"

Hermie glanced over and looked even more impressed. "Remarkable. Absolutely remarkable. So… you know about us then?"

Dad nodded and Hermie's face lit up.

"I must tell the others. It's amazing. Usually we

13

meet with such resistance, suspicion. People think we're delusional or living in fantasy land."

"Not here in Osbury you won't," said Dad. "We know the legends about this place and were hoping that you'd be back some day. I hope that you'll consider Zodiac Lodge as your second home. We are honoured to have you here."

Hermie looked surprised but delighted. "It is rare to find such a welcome so that's very kind of you sir. Most kind."

All this time, I'd been waiting for Hermie to notice *me*. I was Zodiac Girl after all, not Dad, and at last he turned away from his fascination with Dad's bookshelves, pulled a parcel out of the inside pocket in his jacket and looked at me. "Am I right in thinking that you are Miss Thebe Battye?"

I could hardly breathe. "Yes. That's me," I whispered.

He handed me a package. "Then this is for you."

I felt myself blush as I took the parcel and was about to open it when there was a commotion in the hall, and moments later the door opened and Mum burst in looking her usual elegant self in a navy suit and filling the room with the scent of her expensive French perfume. She took one look at Hermie and her face broke into a wide grin showing her gleaming white teeth (she'd had them whitened last month by a top cosmetic dentist.) "Oh lord. You're here! And *so* handsome."

"Estella, this is Hermie," said Dad. "And Hermie, this is my wife Estella."

Mum shook her head from side to side. She was still beaming. "Benjamin thought it might be today. I got back as soon as I could. Oh lord but this is *exciting*. Isn't this exciting, Thebe?" she asked without even glancing at me. She couldn't take her eyes off Hermie. "Now Hermie, honey. You know who we are? What we do? Did Benjamin explain?"

"Erm... I'm starting to get an idea," said Hermie with a grin.

"Battye's the name, astrology's our game," said Mum and she did a little skippy dance. "Oo-ee, I can't resist a moment longer. I have to give you a hug." She went over and embraced Hermie who didn't seem to mind at all. "Welcome. Welcome here. Benjamin, have you given him the guided tour of the house?"

Dad shook his head. "He only just got here a few seconds ago, Estella."

"You been offered some refreshment, Hermie?" asked Mum. "Would you like some lunch?"

"I've had lunch thanks, but a drink would be great," replied Hermie.

Mum turned to me. "Thebe darling, be a sweetheart."

I put my package down even though I was dying to

see what was in it. "What would you like?"

"Oh, just fix a tray, bring everything," said Mum, her eyes still fixed on Hermie. "And use the best cups. The bone china ones if you can find them. Thebe's a dream child. A typical Virgo. She keeps this house running don't you love?" I was about to say "yes", but Mum continued over me. "She's so organized and tidy. The rest of us would forget to eat if she didn't do the weekly internet shop. Oh yes, that child is a marvel. Now run along, love, and fix a tray while your dad and I chat to Hermes here."

"Anything you don't like Hermie?" I asked.

"Not really… oh, except honey. Don't bring me any honey, I… it has a strange effect on me…"

"Like an allergy?" asked Mum. "I'm that way about wheat."

Hermie nodded. "Sort of. All us planets are… um, allergic to honey."

"Think I read that in one of my books, Hermie," said Dad. "How does the allergy manifest?"

"Um… er… let's just say, best to be avoided."

"Sugar okay?" I asked.

Hermie nodded and smiled. "Sugar's fine."

I went into the kitchen but I felt miffed. According to the book, Hermie was my guardian, not theirs. The book said nothing about Zodiac *parents*! But then I couldn't stay mad at them for long. Of course they were as excited as I was. Astrology was their whole life, their passion, and to be meeting one of the planets in the flesh was like meeting their pin-up or Hollywood hero. Plus they were useless in the kitchen. Like Mum may be ace at business but ask her to cook and she's a disaster. Once she flavoured a simple jerk-chicken recipe with sugar instead of salt and another time, she put salt in the banana bread instead of sugar. Hopeless. Her mind is too busy wheeling and dealing. And Dad's no better. He can't even boil an egg. Pat used to help but then she discovered boys and working in the kitchen ruins her nails.

So it's up to me. I took over when I was ten. First thing I did was get a cleaner and housekeeper to come in a couple of days a week and cook up some meals for the freezer, and I do the weekly shop on the internet. I'm a whiz on the computer and I enjoy getting it sorted. And one of my favourite things is organizing the food cupboards so that everything can be easily found. It makes me feel happy when things are in the right places and things are done properly, like I had a little ritual for doing a tray: drinks first, food second, crockery and cutlery last. I poured a jug of pineapple orange drink for our guest, then I got the banana and coconut cake from the cake tin. I knew it was made with sugar not honey because I'd cut the recipe out of a magazine and given the recipe to the housekeeper myself. Last touch was to arrange plates, glasses and napkins on the tray, then I took them all in.

Mum, Dad, Hermie and Pat were sitting on the sofas. Even Cosmo was in there, happily curled up on Hermie's knee! Pat didn't appear to be saying much. She was saying a lot with her body language though. There was an article about speaking without words in my last month's *Girl in the City* magazine. I could tell by the way that Pat was sitting, with her skirt hitched high and her body leaning forward, that she was saying, "Hello, handsome. Let's go for a ride on your motorbike." Not that Mum or Dad noticed that their daughter was flirting so blatantly right in front of them. They only had eyes for Hermie. They were like two teens who had met their boy-band crush and were sitting on the edge of the sofa, hanging on his every word.

"Ah*em*," I coughed to let them know that I was back. Me. The Zodiac Girl. But no one noticed. As usual, I was the invisible member of our family. I put down the tray and went over to the desk where I'd left my package. As the others chatted away and quaffed down the juice and ate the cake, I unwrapped my parcel. Inside were two packets, one smaller than the other. I opened that one first. Inside was a small jewellery box and in that was a silver chain with a tiny silver lady holding a sheaf of wheat. I'd seen pendants like this before as Mum had loads manufactured to sell on the internet site, but this was exceptionally beautiful and delicate. I knew that the sheaf of wheat that the tiny lady was holding was supposed to symbolize wisdom. I glanced up to see if anyone had noticed that I was unwrapping my presents, but they were all still engrossed in their mutual admiration club so I opened the second parcel. Inside was the most divine mobile phone. It was navy with a sprinkling of glitter and at the top was a huge sapphire. It was stunning. I decided to butt into the conversation. "Hermie, thank you so much for my gorgeous presents."

"They're yours as Zodiac Girl, Thebe. And the phone is so that you can get in touch with me and me with you."

At this point, I noticed Pat perk up even more. "Oh really. Can I have a look, Thebe?"

Reluctantly I handed the phone over.

"Oh my!" said Mum when she saw it. "It's lovely. We do a range of phones for each sign but nothing as pretty as that. You must let me know your supplier. And it's interesting that it's blue with the sapphire. All the books seem to say something different about what the stone is for each sign. So much contradiction – like for Virgos, some books and websites say that navy is their colour and others say green or shades of yellow. And some say sapphire is their birthstone and others say agate. What do you think Hermie, sugar?"

And they were off again. I had wanted to ask Hermie the same question that Mum had, but I had also wanted to say that I was glad my special phone had a sapphire on it as that was my favourite stone and blue was my favourite colour. But get a word in with this lot? No way. My special day? The beginning of my special month?

It so wasn't meant to be like this.

Chapter Three

Surprise

"Are you Zodiac Girl because your dad's a famous astrologer?" asked my best mate, Rachel, later that day as we sat on a bench and put our skates on at the local ice rink. I'd told her all about the visit and my Zodiac presents and she was well impressed.

"No. It has nothing to do with Dad, or Mum for that matter," I said as I glanced out at the skaters flying by on the rink in front of us, "although you'd hardly know it the way they took over the whole visit."

"Can I be a Zodiac Girl then?"

"Maybe one day. There's a different one each month somewhere on the planet and it depends on what's coming up in your horoscope. Hermie said that everyone reacts differently and some girls make the most of their time while others choose to ignore it altogether. He said they had one girl who stomped on her Zodiac phone and broke it. I can't imagine doing that as mine is so gorgeous. I'll show you in school tomorrow."

"Have you used it yet?"

"No. And I can only use it to get in touch with Hermie and the planet people and he will use it to get in touch with me. It's like my hotline to them."

"What happens next then?"

"I'm not sure, but it's going to be wonderful. Dad said that he thinks that girls get chosen to be Zodiac Girls when they are at a crossroads or turning point in their lives. I'm not expecting any big changes in my life any time soon, but who knows? Before he left, Hermie said that as Uranus features strongly in my chart that I should expect some kind of surprise. Uranus is the planet of the unexpected and sometimes when he's around things can happen out of the blue like a bolt of lightning, so really anything could happen."

"Wow. How exciting! I so wish I was a Zodiac Girl," said Rachel as she stood up and made her way onto the ice.

"So do I," I called after her, "but I promise I'll tell you all about it so you won't be left out and maybe you can meet Hermie one day."

"That would be so cool," said Rachel and she pushed off the edge and skated perfectly into the centre of the rink.

I felt bad about not being able to share being Zodiac Girl with her as, apart from ice skating which is Rachel's thing, we shared everything. Clothes, jewellery, music, magazines. Her star sign was Cancer so I resolved to get her a Cancerian pendant from Mum's stock and also a mobile phone cover from a new range that Mum had designed. It wouldn't be the same as having the real thing but would be close enough so that Rachel wouldn't feel excluded.

"Come on," she called to me.

I took a deep breath. I'd been dreading this moment. I was total rubbish at ice-skating. I'd tried it a couple of times when Rachel had first got into it and I had fallen flat on my back both times. The only reason I was giving it another shot was that Dad's chosen celebrity for the month was Janet Johnson, the ice-skating champion, and she had invited my whole family to a party at the rink in four weeks time. As Mum and Dad and Pat are all confident skaters, I didn't want to be seen as the family failure, nor did I want to let Dad down.

I wobbled my way onto the rink and gingerly put my feet onto the ice. Immediately I felt my lower half slide away but caught myself just in time and held onto the barrier surrounding the rink.

"Come on," Rachel called again.

"Mff," I mumbled. I was finding it hard to breath. There were too many people on the rink and they were going so fast, whizzing past each other at a million miles an hour. *What if I fall?* I asked myself. *One* of them might skate by and slice my fingers off with the blades of their skates.

Rachel skated towards me. "You okay?" she asked.

I shook my head. "No. I can't do it. I'm sorry. I just can't."

She held out her arm to me. "Hold on to me, you'll be fine. I won't let you fall."

She was looking at me with such encouragement but I couldn't do it. I couldn't let go. I felt like the ice. Frozen. "I can't Rachel, I'm sorry."

"I was the same first time," she said. "It gets easier, it really does. Just try a little way, you can keep holding onto the side."

I still couldn't do it. My legs wouldn't move, I felt a huge knot in my stomach and was finding it hard to breathe.

"Next time," I wheezed. "I promise, I'll do it next time."

Rachel's such a great mate. She didn't push it. She just squeezed my arm. "You'll get there. You'll see. It just takes time."

I staggered off the ice and back to the safety of a nearby bench where my breath slowed down to normal. I couldn't get the skates off fast enough. I sat and watched Rachel and the others for a while and felt miserable. *I'll have to come up with some excuse for getting out of the party*, I thought. *Pretend I have a cold or flu or*

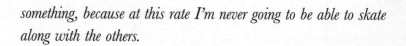

something, because at this rate I'm never going to be able to skate along with the others.

When I got home later, I went downstairs to see what the others were doing. Dad was having a doze on the sofa in the study with his headphones on and Mum was at the other end of the sofa, working on her laptop. The French windows were open and a warm breeze wafted through from the garden.

"Hey hon," she said without looking up from the screen when I walked in. "How was the skating?"

"Fine," I lied. "Um... what you doing?"

"I'm preparing a press release to say that the planets are here in human form and that one of them visited us here today."

"No! *No*, Mum! You mustn't do that."

"Why ever not baby? This is the opportunity of a lifetime. Just think of the business it's going to bring us."

My head filled with a series of horrible images. People teasing me at school for a start. It was one thing telling Rachel about being a Zodiac Girl, but if it got around school, I'd be the laughing stock. My family stood out as unusual as it was and I had wised up pretty fast to the fact that not everyone believed in the stars, and that some people even thought it was complete nonsense and that only wackos believed in it. If it got out that my family thought that the planets were here in human form, people would think we really were bananas. No. It mustn't happen. Plus the fact that Hermie and the rest of the planets must feel free to come and go at our house. The last thing they'd want was to be hounded by paparazzi.

"Dad. *Dad*. Wake up," I said and tugged on Dad's toes until he opened his eyes. He took off his headphones and sat up.

"What's going on?" he asked.

"It's Mum. You have to stop her. She wants to tell the press that the planets are here in human form. I... I don't think we should tell anyone."

Dad shook his head. "Estella, Thebe's right on this one. Let it go."

"But baby..."

"No. We don't want the planet people to feel uncomfortable coming here now do we? We want this to be a haven for them so we're going to keep it quiet. In the family. The press would treat them like freaks. It's a no-no."

Mum stuck out her bottom lip like a five year old.

"Come on now, you know we're right," said Dad.

Mum folded her arms over her stomach and pouted even more. She didn't like not getting her own way.

"I don't often put my foot down Estella, but I'm going to about this. We are hosts for the honoured guests and that's it. Just having them here will be wonderful and think what we can learn. It can help business that way and maybe even give us more ideas for merchandising but *no* press and that's final."

I glanced over at Mum to see how she was going to react. She'd gone all coy and girly and was looking up at Dad from under her eyelashes. "Oh Benjie," she said. "I do *love* it when you're forceful."

Oh for God's sake, I thought. *I hope they don't start kissing in front of me. That would be so disgusting.*

"You hear me Estella, I mean it," said Dad, clearly relishing the effect he was having on Mum.

"Oh I hear you Mr Battye, you big lug you," she said then she clapped her hands. "We'll have lots of tea parties for them. Dinner parties. Thebe love, invite them all over as soon as you can. We can get Nikkya to cater so that they can sample authentic Caribbean food. What do you think? Thebe, be sure to find out if any of them are vegetarian or have any special dietary needs apart from that honey thing." (Aunt Nikkya has her own restaurant that serves delicious Caribbean food, the kind Mum used to make before she became Business Woman of the Year. We ordered supper from Auntie at least once a week usually.)

Dad and I looked at each other and smiled. Mum was off again but at least it was in a safe direction this time.

"But Mum, I don't know how it works exactly. I don't even know if I'll get to meet all ten planets. Hermie said most Zodiac Girls got to meet the ones who are prevalent in their charts."

"So look at your chart, child. What are you waiting for?"

"I am waiting for Hermie, my guardian, to contact me to tell me what's next. He said something about Uranus but that was all…, but you're right, we should be able to work out some of what's coming up for me by ourselves."

Dad got my chart down from where he'd blu-tacked it on the wall near his desk and the three of us bent over it.

"Hmm, looks like some conflict coming up, munchkin," said Dad. "Uranus, yes we know about that – a surprise on its way – although that could have been the fact that you got to be Zodiac Girl, that's a surprise. What else? Hmm, the Moon, yes, emotions stirred up, but then the Moon always does that."

"Yes but nothing major?" I asked.

"Talking about conflict," said Mum, as she suddenly lost interest in my chart and picked up another one that

THEBE'S CHART

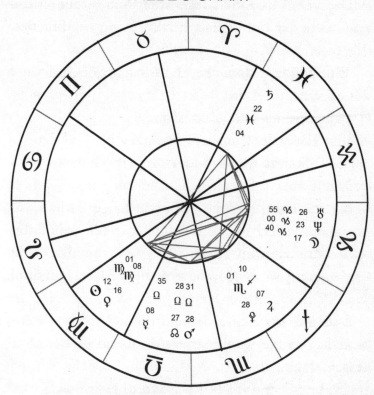

SYMBOLS OF THE PLANETS AND SIGNS

☉	☽	☿	♀		♈	♉	♊	♋	♌
SUN	MOON	MERCURY	VENUS		ARIES	TAURUS	GEMINI	CANCER	LEO

♂	♃	♄	♅		♍	♎	♏	✗
MARS	JUPITER	SATURN	URANUS		VIRGO	LIBRA	SCORPIO	SAGGITARIUS

♆	♇		♑	♒	♓
NEPTUNE	PLUTO		CAPRICORN	AQUARIUS	PISCES

was lying in Dad's in tray. "You seen this?"

Dad looked over. "Your sister's chart."

Mum nodded. "Now that's what I call conflict.

Mars, Venus and the Moon well squared up against each other. I think she's finally going to split with Norrece."

Dad nodded. "I saw his chart too. It does indicate a rift of sorts."

"Understatement," said Mum.

"Er, Earth to Mum and Dad. Zodiac Girl here," I said. "I thought we were looking at *my* chart."

Mum waved the air as if dismissing me. "No hon, you got it right. Hermie will be in touch. How about you go and check the kitchen supplies while your father and I discuss my sister? If we're going to be entertaining, we need to have plenty of food and drink in."

I sighed. For a brief second there, I thought I was actually going to be the centre of attention. But no. It was a shame that Aunt Mattie and Uncle Norrece might break up though. I was sad to hear that. I liked them both but it was true, they did argue a lot. They were both Leos. Leo is the sign of the lion and anyone born in that month likes to be king of the jungle which is hard if there are two of you both battling for the place. Leos can also roar like lions and boy it was noisy when those two were over and not getting on. However, like all Leos, they also had big hearts and were very generous and that made up for all the growling. They had a daughter, Yasmin, and as much as Uncle

Norrece and Auntie Mattie could be charm personified, Yasmin was misery on a stick. She was fifteen and bossy and sullen unless you were a boy, in which case she suddenly became Little Miss Sunshine. She was a Gemini and they can be very flirty. She called me Miss Prissy Knickers just because she came across me colour-coding my wardrobe one rainy afternoon when they were visiting. When I tried to explain that it was so that I could find things easily, she said, "Oh get a life, loser." I hate her. With a bit of luck, if Auntie Mattie and Norrece do split up, Yasmin will get sent somewhere far away and I'll never have to see her ever again. Somewhere like Australia. Or the Moon.

"Hey Dad. How do you think the Sun is manifested down here?" I asked. "I forgot to ask Hermie who they were all here and what they did."

"Oh, we asked him when you were in the kitchen," said Mum.

"And you didn't tell me! Mu-*um*. I am the Zodiac Girl you know, not you."

Mum chuckled and tickled me under the chin. "Oo, you's so sweet when you're cross. Isn't she cute when she's cross, Benjamin?"

Dad began tickling me too and soon I was across one of the sofas laughing and gasping for breath. I am the most ticklish person in the world. "Just *tell* me what the other planets are, Dad," I gasped as they let me go.

"Erm, let me remember. Okay. Hermie—"

"Motorbike messenger," I said.

"Correct," said Dad. "Venus. Now tell me about Venus, Thebe?"

I sighed. This is how I got to know everything I did about astrology – Dad turned every simple question into an opportunity to teach me a lesson. "Venus rules Taureans and Librans and is the planet of love and beauty," I replied.

"Correct. And she runs a beauty salon in Osbury and in the evenings she runs classes in how to discover your inner goddess."

"Cool," I said and got a piece of paper from Dad's desk on which to write the planet people down.

"She should run a dating agency," said Mum. "If we meet her, I'm going to tell her. It would be perfect for her."

"Er, Mum, I think they are here to tell us, that is me, what to do, not the other way around."

"Says who? There are no rules. Did Hermie give you a set of rules?"

"No Mum. Do Mars next, Dad. And before you ask, Mars is the ruler of Aries, god of war."

"Ex-marine, teaches classes in karate and self-defence," said Dad.

"Brilliant, obvious," I said as I added Mars to my list.

"See if you can guess the next one, hon," said

Mum. "Let's do… Jupiter."

"Planet of jollity and expansion rules Sagittarius," I said. "Hmm. Clown?"

Mum shook her head.

"Caterer?"

"Close," said Dad. "He runs a deli in Osbury. Venus is called Nessa down here by the way, and he's called Joe."

"Okay. Let's guess for Uranus," I said. "Rules Aquarius, planet of the unexpected and magic. Hmm, magician?"

"Again, not a bad guess, Thebe," said Dad. "He runs a magic shop and a cyber café. He's called Uri and he's also in Osbury. I just knew they'd all be around here somewhere."

"So who's left then?" asked Mum.

"The Moon, Sun, Neptune, Saturn and Pluto," I said.

"Saturn, the taskmaster. He's here as a Dr Cronus, a headmaster," said Dad.

"Perfect," I said as I wrote that down.

"Pluto, the planet of transformation," said Dad. "He's an interior designer. Neptune, Lord of dreams and King of the sea, he runs a fish and chip shop and I do believe owns a couple of boats and takes tourists out for day trips."

Our discussion was cut short by the sound of the

phone ringing. Mum picked up and I could tell by the expression on her face that it was bad news. After a few minutes, she put the phone down and turned to face us.

"As I thought. Mattie and Norrece are going their separate ways. At least for a while."

"What are they going to do?" asked Dad.

"Take a bit of time out to think things over. She's going to stay with relatives in Jamaica. He's going to an island in Greece to chill out and think about what he wants."

"Yasmin going with her mother?" asked Dad.

Mum shook her head. "You know you can't just swan off from school in the middle of term. Plus they don't want her getting behind. They've asked if she can stay here. It's just for a month."

"A month!" I blurted. *An hour with Yasmin here would be enough to drive me insane,* I thought.

"Uh-huh. A month. So Thebe, hon, you got the biggest room so she's going to have to go in with you."

"*Me?* But what about the spare room?"

Mum and Dad both cracked up. The "spare" room which had been done out as the Saturn room was anything but spare at the moment. It was stuffed as high as the ceiling with merchandise samples for Mum's business, plus anything else that we couldn't place elsewhere – bikes, old toys, rollerblades, books, old clothes and shoes in black bin bags. It was like a charity shop in there and you could hardly get the door open, it was so full. Tidying it up and having a good throw out was on my "to do" list.

"We could empty it," I said. "We've been meaning to make it into a proper spare room for months."

"We could," Mum agreed, "but she's coming tomorrow. We'd never get it done by then. Besides, where would we put all the stuff? The garage is piled high too."

"Why can't she go in with Pat?"

"Because this is Pat's GCSE year and the loft room doesn't have space for another bed. Plus she needs space and quiet to study and you have a spare bed in your room."

It was true. I had a bed in there for when Rachel stayed for a sleepover. I was just scanning my mind for any other alternative (like a tent in the garden!) when my zodiac phone bleeped that I had a text.

"Oo, it's the Zodiamobile," said Mum. "Let's see. Let's see."

I quickly had a look in the hope that it might be some *good* news.

"Surprises aren't always what you think, love Uri," said the text.

Dad cracked up laughing. "Can't argue with that then, can you munchkin?" he asked. "And Uranus is also the planet of the rebel as well as the planet of surprises. Now are you going to go all rebellious on us?"

Mum laughed too but I couldn't join in with them. *No. No. NO. NOOOOOOOOOOOOOOOO,* I thought. *Yasmin coming to stay can't be my surprise. It is my zodiac month. It's supposed to be the best month ever. There has to be some kind of mistake.*

Chapter Four

Room mate from Hell

<u>Thebe's list of things to do</u>
Tidy room and get Mrs W to make up
bed for Yasmin.
  Put flowers and fruit next to her bed
to make her welcome.
  Call Hermie to synchronize diaries for
my zodiac month.
  Do homework.
  Practise ice-skating.

"And that scraggy thing can think again about coming in here," said Yasmin as she picked up Cosmo and shoved him out into the hall. He looked up at me accusingly and I tried to communicate by telepathy that I was sorry. It wasn't my decision. He wasn't appeased. He looked how I felt. Disgruntled. He padded off down the corridor towards Mum and Dad's room with his tail down. It wasn't fair. Yasmin'd only been in my room ten minutes and already she was taking over.

"His *name* is Cosmo and he always sleeps in here," I protested. "It's *his* home."

"Bu… uh, I'm allergic, a…a…chooo," said Yasmin in a totally fake bunged up voice. I knew bunged up when I heard it because I genuinely suffered from allergies. Pollen. Wheat. Dust. All sorts of things brought it on (although luckily cats isn't one of them), and Yasmin was clearly putting the snuffles on to get her own way. She just didn't like cats.

Next thing she did was to go to the wardrobe and pull out five hangers with my clothes on. She laid them over the back of my desk chair.

"But… but I already made some space for you," I said as I indicated the free area to the right of my clothes.

"I'm *fifteen*. I have more clothes than you. Us older girls need more than little girls," she said as she went back to her bed, opened her suitcase and turned it upside down so that stuff spilt out onto the mattress then onto the floor. She put a few things away and then she began to pile books from the bookshelf next to my desk on to the floor.

"What are you doing?" I asked as I sat on my bed and watched her.

"Making a line," she replied as she laid the books out like the foundations of a brick wall. When she'd made a line from one side of the room to the other, she stood up and indicated the area on one side of the line. "Now this is my side, yeah?" Then she indicated the side with my bed on. "And that's yours, yeah? No crossing over." She then turned her back on me, threw herself on her bed and put on her iPod headphones. She was clearly no happier about the change in her living arrangements than I was, although earlier in the day I had resolved to make the most of the situation and welcome her to the house. I'd even been out and bought some flowers with my pocket money for the cabinet besides her bed and put a bowl of oranges there for her.

I don't know why I bothered, I thought, as I made myself bite back what was on the tip of my tongue. I was dying to say that actually it was *my* room and she was *my* guest, but Mum had given me a lecture about how Yasmin's parents breaking up must be hard on her and we must all be kind and treat her with kid gloves. I knew what kind of gloves I'd like to treat her with and they weren't kid gloves, they were boxing gloves. I'd like to sock her right in her pretty lipglossed gob. Sometimes I even surprise myself with how violent my thoughts can be.

Suddenly Yasmin took out her headphones and turned towards me. "And what is this room?" she asked as she looked around at the décor. "It's not normal."

My bedroom was the Venus room in the house and Mum and I had decided that seeing as Venus was the goddess of love and beauty, that it should be the most beautiful room in the house. Venus is the second closest planet to the Sun and after the Moon it is the brightest object in the night sky. Venus is also known as the morning or evening star (even though it's a planet!) so when we started decorating, I thought that it was only natural to go with a star theme. We'd painted the walls white, then all around the tops, I'd stencilled in stars. The lamp in the centre of the room was a silver star and the bedspreads were white but the cushions were silver. It looked clean and neat and I loved it.

On the wall between the two beds was a mural that my Auntie Francelle had done (she's the artist in the family and had done a number of the paintings around the house including some in Dad's study – and of course, she works as part of Battye Enterprises and designs cards and posters for Mum.) My mural depicted the goddess Venus with long hair curved around her body. It was actually a copy of a painting I'd seen in a book once by the Italian artist, Sandro Botticelli. It was called the Birth of Venus. I couldn't wait to show it to the real Venus when she turned up which, according to a text that I'd had last night from Hermie, was probably going to be in the next couple of days. Venus and the Moon, he'd said. He also indicated that there was to be a difficult aspect, but that was to be expected with old grumpy boots Yasmin turning up. I really hoped that the Moon and Venus would come over in person like Hermie had. That would be so cool.

"That is naff," said Yasmin pointing to the mural. She got up from the bed and picked up a roll of paper from her things on the floor. "In fact, seeing as some of the wall on which it's painted comes over my side of the room, I'm going to put this over it." She unrolled a poster of a huge red pair of lips with a tongue sticking out; underneath it, it said "People Suck". She blu-tacked it to the wall.

"Nooo," I said. "That looks awful there. Please. Be reasonable. And it covers up Auntie Francelle's work."

Yasmin shrugged. "So bite me," she said. "Your mum said we had to share and that we had to be nice to each other right? I'm going through a life trauma so you've got to go easy on me. Right?"

She had me. "Right but… can't you see it just doesn't go with the rest of the room."

Yasmin laughed. "Since when have you been Queen of Interior Design? Your mum said to make myself at home and that's what I'm doing. Would you like me to go and tell her that you're making me feel unwelcome?"

"No, course not." *Maybe I am being a tad unwelcoming,*

I thought and I resolved to be kinder. I knew I wouldn't like it if my mum and dad were splitting up and I had to uproot and go and stay with another family. "I'm sorry. Of course you must have your poster up."

Yasmin smiled. I think she knew that I didn't have a leg to stand on. And then I remembered. I wasn't alone in this. I was Zodiac Girl. The planets were here to help me for my special month. Maybe there was a message of support or some advice from Hermie as to how to deal with my new room-mate. I went to my desk (which was only just over my side) and got my zodiac phone from the drawer.

Yasmin immediately perked up. "What's that?"

"Erm. A phone."

"I can see that. Where did you get it?"

"Oh. Don't know. It was a present. It's for my birth sign."

Yasmin nodded. "It's cool. Could your mum get me one like it?"

"Doubt it," I said, "and anyhow, you're not a Virgo like me so one in this colour and the stone on it wouldn't be right for your sign. You're Gemini and—"

"Like I care one bit about that tosh," Yasmin interrupted, "but it is a cool phone. Give me a look."

I passed the phone to her and she pressed a few buttons and turned it over. "Doesn't seem to be working."

"It was working earlier," I said and I prayed that she hadn't pressed something wrong and broken it.

She tossed it back to me. "Not much use if it doesn't work," she said, and then she pulled out some small speakers from her pile on the floor. She plugged her iPod into them and the room filled up with really LOUD, head-banging music. She sat back down on her bed and gave me a smug smile. "Cool sounds, hey?"

I winced. "Not a word I'd have used to describe it," I said, and I began to tidy up my side of the room in the hope that she might see my good example and learn from it.

Yasmin laughed. "Jeez Thebe, anyone ever told you that you're like an old lady?" she asked as she reached out, took an orange and lay back against the cushions as she began to peel it. When she had done, she threw the peel onto the floor and began to pop segments of the orange into her mouth.

I stepped over the line of books, picked up the peel and put it into the bin under my desk. In response, Yasmin turned her music up even higher.

I looked my phone over and pressed the button that Hermie had told me to use in order to reach him. It seemed to be working again. I texted my message.

"Please help. Urgent. Cousin come to stay. Not friendly. What shall I do?"

A message bleeped right back.

"Mercury has gone retrograde. Hermie is unavailable at the moment. Call back later."

Oh no, I thought. I knew what Mercury going retrograde meant. It happened regularly throughout the year, usually three times, but I so hoped that it didn't mean that I wasn't going to be able to get hold of my guardian on the very month that I was Zodiac Girl. That would be so unfair. Like winning the lottery but finding out that you'd lost the winning ticket. I went downstairs to see if Dad might be able to shed any light on the situation.

"Dad, Mercury's gone retrograde," I said as I burst into his study to find that there was someone with him. "Oh sorry, I didn't realize that you had company." Sitting opposite Dad was a man with a big silver-grey beard and a smiley weather-beaten face. He was wearing a sea captain's hat and a smart navy blazer. Dad and he were drinking beers.

"Ah! Is this the Zodiac Girl?" asked the man.

I nodded and looked to Dad for explanation. Dad grinned. "Thebe, meet Captain John Dory."

"Oh hi, Captain Jo –"

"Also known as Neptune!" said Dad.

"No kidding? Wow! Hi. I…" I went over to the wall and glanced at my chart. There didn't seem to be any strong link to Neptune happening that I could see, and

Hermie hadn't mentioned anything about a visit from Captain John in his earlier texts.

"So how's your time as Zodiac Girl going, Thebe?" asked the Captain.

"Oh. Fine I guess. Early days. Er… but I wasn't expecting you. It's not in my chart at the moment. I was expecting Venus and the Moon. What are you doing here?"

Dad frowned at me as if I'd said something wrong. "Now then Thebe, all the planets are welcome in this house. It doesn't have to be in your chart for them to pop round. Indeed no. Captain John, you come by anytime."

Captain John raised his glass. "That's good of you, Benjamin," then he turned to me. "And actually all us planets affect your chart, Thebe, you should know that. Yes, some are more prevalent at certain times, but even those in the background have an influence. Now, as far as I remember, you have your Neptune in Capricorn. Know what that means?"

"Er… Neptune's to do with dreams and ideals isn't it? I mean you?"

The Captain nodded. "And in your case, you have very high expectations. High ideals."

I nodded. "Mum always taught us to have goals."

The Captain nodded again. "But make them reasonable ones, Thebe. You might find that you have

45

to lower your expectations here and there."

I nodded back but I was unsure exactly what he meant. Did he mean to do with my being a Zodiac Girl? No way was I going to lower my expectations to do with that. Why should I? Hermie had said that some Zodiac Girls let the opportunity go by and I certainly didn't want that to happen. I wanted to be a girl who made every single moment of it count – which reminded me about Hermie. "So Dad, Mercury has gone retrograde. What will that mean for me as Zodiac Girl? Especially as he's my guardian."

"It will be for about three weeks," said Captain John. "Mercury retrograde usually means miscommunications, misunderstandings of some sort, computers crashing, phones not working, things going missing."

"In my case, it seems to be Hermie himself," I said.

Dad and the Captain nodded.

"Best not to make any important decisions at the moment," said the Captain. "Mercury is all about mental clarity, so when he's retrograde, your judgment can be clouded. Still, it's only for three weeks."

"Three weeks! But it can't be. I mean, surely, that can't be right. I mean… will he be around at all?" I blustered.

Captain John shrugged. "Maybe, maybe not. You can never be certain of anything when Mercury goes retrograde."

I glanced over at the Captain. I really wanted some time alone with Dad to discuss my chart and make plans for how best to make use of my time. "Er… Dad…"

Dad took a sip of his beer. "Just go with the flow, baby," he said, then turned his attention back to his visitor. "Just go with the flow and all will be well, and in the meantime the Captain here and I have a lot of things to talk about, so be a dear and run along hey?"

"Good advice – to go with the flow," said Captain John. "And Thebe, believe in your dreams."

Pff, I thought as I left the room. *Go with the flow? Run along. Hah! What did Dad know? I can't "flow" back up to my room, which is what I'd really like to do, because it's too noisy in there with my room-mate from hell.* I kicked the wall with frustration.

"Ow!" I cried as my toe throbbed with pain. I went up the stairs to the first floor and listened at my bedroom door. Yasmin was still playing music at full volume in there. I went up the next flight of stairs. Maybe I could hang out in Pat's room and read a book. Her door was locked. I knocked. "Pat. You in there?"

"Go away," came her voice from inside.

"Please," I said. "I won't get in your way."

"You've got your own room."

"Haven't. Yasmin's taken over."

"Then go and see what Mum's doing. I'm busy."

I sighed and set off back down the stairs and along to Mum and Dad's bedroom which was the Aquarius room. When I opened the door, I saw that the silver velvet curtains were closed, the only light coming from a lavender scented candle on Mum's dressing table, and some gentle New Age music was playing. It felt cool and peaceful in there. The walls were painted electric blue. Mum and I had done some stencilling along the top of the walls similar to my room only instead of stars we'd done a series of silver streaks of lightning. These symbolized the energy of Uranus, the ruling planet of Aquarius, which was often said to come like a bolt out of the blue. Mum was lying on the bed in her dressing gown and looked like something out of a horror movie. Her hair was scraped back in a hair band, her face was plastered white and she had a cucumber slices over both eyes.

"Mum…" I whispered.

"Erf. Oo ee it?"

"Thebe."

"Erf 'ace 'ack odge," she said through her closed mouth. I understood. Face pack. She didn't like to say much when she had one on in case it cracked.

"Can I stay in here for a while?"

"Uh uh," she said as she shook her head from side

to side. Mum took her chilling time *very* seriously. I got the message.

Not wanted upstairs. Not wanted downstairs. Not wanted in my own room, I thought as I trooped down to the kitchen. Outside it was pouring with rain so the garden wasn't an option. *Go with the flow, Dad had said. What blooming flow? I'm the only one who really understands what it takes to keep things flowing. I really am*, I thought, as I stomped off into the utility room at the back of the kitchen to put the dirty washing into the light and dark piles ready for Mrs Watson who was coming in tomorrow morning. *If this family went with the flow, there would be no food, no dinner, no clean clothes. The house would be a total mess if it wasn't for me getting things organized!*

Above the dryer was one of Mum's charts listing all the signs of the zodiac and the symbol for that sign.

Aries: the ram.
Taurus: the bull.
Gemini: the twins.
Cancer: the crab.
Leo: the lion.
Virgo: the virgin.
Libra: the scales.
Scorpio: the scorpion.
Sagittarius: the archer.
Capricorn: the goat.

Aquarius: the water carrier.

Pisces: two fish.

It was a nice poster with illustrations of each symbol drawn by Auntie Francelle but I stuck my tongue out at it. I felt cross. Being part of a zodiac family, living in a zodiac house and being a Zodiac Girl wasn't any fun at all!

From one of Dad's books on astrology:

The word *retrograde* applies, in astrology, to the *apparent* backward motion through the zodiac of a planet. All the planets, except the Sun and Moon, have these retrograde periods, but Mercury is most famous for them, probably because Mercury represents communication.

This includes writing, speaking, shopping and signing contracts. While Mercury is retrograde, don't give that party, be extra careful what you say and what you interpret when chatting with or writing to friends, expect mail to take longer than usual and computers to crash, so make sure you back up anything important.

Good things to do when Mercury is retrograde are: chill out, meditate, edit the book/poem/song/essay you've been writing, clean house, talk to your pet, listen to music, paint, catch up on sleep!

Chapter Five

Queen of Sheba

"You're telling me that nothing's happened?" asked Rachel the next day at school when I told her about my first weekend as a Zodiac Girl. She looked as disappointed as I felt. "I thought you'd have been having a fantastic time with all sorts of magical things happening."

"Maybe that's how it is for some Zodiac Girls but not for this one, Thebe Battye. I must be so uninspiring and ordinary that the planets can't even be bothered to think of anything exciting for me to do and even my guardian's cleared off, he's so bored."

"You're not boring, Thebe," said Rachel and she gave my arm a squeeze. "I think you're the most interesting girl in the whole school." Rachel has been my best friend since junior school. Dad used to call us Ebony and Ivory after a song written by Paul McCartney who was Dad's favourite Beatle. It's something to do with piano keys I think. The lyrics are "Ebony and ivory play together in perfect harmony," or something like that. We're total opposite in looks as Rachel is tall with long blonde hair and creamy white skin and I'm small and dark with coffee-coloured skin.

I smiled. It was nice of her to say that but what I knew she really meant was that my *family* was interesting and where I *lived* was interesting. I was only interesting because I basked in their reflection. It was only a matter of time before she realized that I was the black sheep of the family. I was the dull one.

After school, I went up to the ice rink to try and get a bit of practise in without anyone I knew witnessing my shame, but for all my best intentions, I still couldn't let go of the edge or stand up on my own. I made my way home afterwards feeling like a failure and hoped that I could get my room to myself for half an hour before Yasmin got back from her school. I was hoping to tidy up and get the room organized after the mess she'd made everywhere, as seeing everything neat and tidy always made me feel better again.

I let myself in and was about to go and make a peanut and raspberry jam sandwich (with rye bread as I'm allergic to wheat) when I heard the sound of laughter and chattering coming from Dad's study. I knocked on the door in case he had a client with him but there was no response and the laughter continued. In the end, my curiosity got the better of me so I opened the door and stuck my head around. Captain

John Dory was back, but this time, he had someone else with him. He was much older looking than the Captain, had a long white beard, wore little glasses and was dressed in an old-fashioned looking tweed suit. He was engrossed in one of Dad's old books. And then it dawned on me. *If Captain John Dory was here. Maybe the other man was one of the planet people too.*

"Ah, here she is," said Dad when he spotted me. "Come on in, Thebe. We've got guests!"

Mum bustled in from behind me with a tray of drinks and a big smile. "Sorry guys, it's cranberry and apple juice as we haven't got any nectar of the gods today. Maybe next time."

The guests cracked up laughing like Mum had said the funniest thing ever.

"Thebe, come in. Meet everyone," said Dad. "Captain John Dory, you know. And this is Dr Cronus a.k.a. Saturn." The man in glasses nodded in my direction.

I did my best to smile in a friendly manner but I wasn't sure what to say or how to be. How to greet planets manifest in human form hadn't been covered at our school. I felt like I was going to faint or my brain was going to short circuit. And then I remembered what a mess the Saturn room was upstairs. I so hoped that Mum and Dad hadn't shown him up there or else he might have got upset.

"Er, have you had the grand tour of the house?" I

asked, trying to sound casual.

"Ground floor only," Dr Cronus replied. "My old bones can't do the stairs like I used to."

Thank heavens for that, I thought. *Still it's strange that he's in here with Neptune and Dad and doesn't seem that bothered about talking to me. I remember that Hermie mentioned something about Saturn in my chart before he took off, but I don't remember him saying anything about Neptune, so what's he doing here? I know. Maybe he's come over to make up for Hermie disappearing and he's come with Dr Cronus to introduce themselves and congratulate me on being a Zodiac Girl.*

However, it wasn't just the fact that they were there that was making me feel unsettled, it was the atmosphere in the room. It was like there had been a surge in electricity or someone had turned on the heating to full blast. The room felt like it was bubbling with an energy that was so alive that it seemed that it might blast the walls down.

"Er... no Hermie?" I asked.

"Retrograde," chorused everyone then they all laughed again.

"Now Thebe, I'm sure you have homework to do," said Dad.

"Yes. It's very important to do your homework," said Dr Cronus and he gave me a stern look over his glasses. I remembered that Mum had said that Saturn was the taskmaster of the zodiac, the one who taught

54

important lessons, and that his human guise was that of a headmaster. I could see that he'd be a very strict one and was glad that he wasn't at my school.

"I always do my homework," I told him. I did. I was an A-grade pupil and was never late with work. It was important to me to always be the best if I could, both at home and at school.

Dr Cronus observed me for a few moments which made me feel more uncomfortable than ever, then he turned away as if he'd lost interest. *Oh god, he can see how dull I am*, I thought as I tugged on Mum's arm. At first she took no notice as she seemed intent on chatting with the guests but eventually, she gave in and came out with me to the corridor.

"What is it, Thebe?" she asked.

"Mum, I'm not sure that both Neptune and Saturn should be here today. Hermie told me that Zodiac Girls only get to meet those who are prevalent in their chart in their special month. I think Saturn is but the only others who are supposed to be here are the Moon and Venus."

Mum patted my head. "Oh chill, Thebe honey, these guys aren't here to see *you*. They're here to see *us*. Your father invited them over to look at his library and to... well, to talk stars. And they seem as eager as we are. Joe Jupiter popped over this afternoon too while you were out at school. They are so interested to find out how astrology is perceived in this day and age and they're dying to see all my merchandise. Now don't you worry your pretty little head about them. You run along upstairs."

There it was again, *run along*. Mum must have seen my face fall because she pointed upstairs. "You have your own guests. Up there."

"Me? Who?"

"What were you just telling me about the Moon and Venus? You were right and they *are* here. Pat took them up and I think Yasmin's home too."

Oh lollipops, the Moon and Venus alone with Pat and Yasmin, yiiiiiiiiiiiiikes, I thought as I took the stairs two at a time and prayed that my sister and my cousin hadn't put my planet guides off for good. I burst into my room to find the kind of scene that you'd find in any girl's bedroom. A woman with long blonde hair had her back to me and was braiding Yasmin's hair while Pat was lolling on my bed. By the way she was holding her hands up she had clearly had her nails done recently.

"Hey, Thebe," said Pat. "This is Nessa. She's come from a beauty salon in – where was it Nessa?"

"Osbury, dahlin'," said the woman in an Essex accent as she turned to me and smiled. She was the most beautiful woman I had ever seen in my life. She had a perfect heart-shaped face, white blonde hair, sky blue eyes and a smile that lit up the room. I was thrown for a moment. Was she Venus? Could she be? She was certainly stunning enough, but would a goddess-type planet person wear tight, white jeans, even if they did have little diamante sequins up the seams? And her T-shirt looked totally up to date, there was nothing ancient about it at all. Somehow though, I'd imagined that Venus would wear goddess-type clothes but the woman in our room was pure footballer's wife trendy. "Hi there, Thebe."

"Are… you… you… Venus?" I whispered.

Yasmin cracked up. "Venus schemus. Der! Time for your medication, Thebe."

Pat rolled her eyes up to the ceiling. "Take no notice, Ness," she said. "My little sister, in fact my whole family, is bonkers about the stars."

"Is that right?" said Nessa and she kept her eyes on me and then winked. I was certain who she was then. And she knew I knew. It didn't matter what my stupid sister said. Or my cousin. Nessa *was* Venus.

"What do you…? That is… do you like the room?" I asked.

Nessa looked around in appreciation. "Bloomin' love it," she said and her glance stopped on the mural that had been partially covered by Yasmin's horrible poster. "Shame you can't see that fab paintin' properly though. Based on a Botticelli, innit?"

I nodded. "The Birth of Venus."

"That's what I thought," said Yasmin, getting up and taking the poster down immediately. "Such a shame not to see all of it."

I couldn't believe how sucky-uppy she was acting. I so wanted Pat and Yasmin to clear out so that I could have a proper talk with Nessa. There were so many things I wanted to ask her but they seemed intent on staying. And stay they did. They talked about hair and make-up and skin care, even how to wax your legs, and Nessa didn't seem to mind at all. She finished Yasmin's hair. She painted Pat's toenails. She showed both of them how to make the most of their lips. She offered to show me how to do make-up too, but I wasn't bothered about that. I had far more important things to ask her about. I felt myself getting cross again. *What was the point of being a Zodiac Girl*, I thought, *if you had to share it with your stupid relatives?*

"Er… is there anyone else with you?" I asked when I suddenly realized that Mum had said something about the Moon having arrived with Venus.

"Oh yeah," said Nessa and she looked around as if expecting someone else to appear out of nowhere. "Selene was wiv us when yer mum gave us the tour of the 'ouse when we first got 'ere. Where'd she go?"

Pat and Yasmin shrugged.

"She asked where the bathroom was," said Pat. "Maybe she's in there."

I set off to look. Maybe the Moon lady would be more interested in *me*. But then again, with my luck, she probably wouldn't.

I found her sitting half way up the stairs to Pat's room. She had the look of a mermaid about her, although without the tail, as I could clearly see two feet with sparkly nails in silver sandals poking out from under her ankle-length skirt. Her clothes were made from a luminous, pale grey-green, silky material, the colour of fish's scales, and she had long silver white hair that fell over her face. She was leaning over with her head in her hands and she didn't look happy at all.

"Erm… are you all right?" I asked as I approached as quietly as I could.

She looked up and I saw that her eyes were the colour of the sea – aquamarine – and the iris was outlined with deep jade green. On her forehead, she had a silver dot. She was very striking but in a different way to Nessa. Nessa was in-your-face obvious gorgeous whereas this woman was gentler looking with a quieter beauty.

"Oh!" she said.

I sat besides her. "I… er… I'm Thebe."

"Oh," she said again. "Zodiac Girl?"

I nodded. "Are you Selene?"

She nodded. "Selene Luna."

"The Moon," I said and then I couldn't think of

anything else to say so we both sat in silence for a few minutes. "Erm… is there something the matter?" Selene sniffed and it was then that I realized that she'd been crying. I put my hand on her arm. "Oh don't cry, it can't be all that bad. What is it? You can tell me. I'm a good listener."

Selene sniffed again and pointed upstairs. "Your mum gave us the tour when we arrived. Beautiful room after beautiful room. The house is… lovely."

"I know. Mum's very proud of the décor. Our house was even featured in *Heavenly Homes* magazine one month. Did you see my room?"

Selene nodded. "Yes…" *sniff, sniff,* "it's really nice. It's… all… lovely…" *Sob, sob.*

"So what is it? Shall I get Mum? She really wanted you all to feel at home here." And then I realized. How could I have been so insensitive? There was no Moon room. It had been painted over. "Oh peanuts! No Moon room. Oh Selene, I am so sorry. There used to be. It was up there and it was lovely, it really was, magical and then… my sister Pat…"

"I know. Painted over it. Ten planets and I'm the only one who got covered over."

"Not exactly. The Saturn room is stuffed to the ceiling with Mum's merchandise and anything that won't fit in any other room."

"Yes but underneath all that, it's still the Saturn

room isn't it? But mine's been removed. Painted over. It happens all the time you know. Like I'm invisible sometimes. People don't realize how hard it is for me. I try my best you know, I really do, I try to shine, I put out as much light as I can but it's never enough. It's because I don't have my *own* light, did you know that? I shine by the sunlight reflected from my surface. Without the Sun, I'm nothing but a cold, rocky place... I am sooooo boring, no wonder your sister painted me out of the picture. It's like everyone's always so bowled over by the Sun or by Venus but the Moon, the Moon, so boring, so dull, hasn't even got her own light..."

It was as if she was describing my exact experience! Poor Selene, I thought. "I *so* know how you feel!" I said.

"Do you? How could you? You're Zodiac Girl and your family, well they're all so fabulous."

"Exactly," I said. "But I'm just like you. They shine but without them, I'm nothing. I'm little Miss Ordinary."

Selene looked at me. "You? Never. Just look at you. You're so pretty, like a toffee-colored cherub with the cutest hair. How do you get it like that?"

I felt a warm glow inside. That was the nicest thing anyone had said to me in ages. "My aunt braids it," I said. "It's called cornrow braiding when they do it close to the head like this because the braids look like sheaves of corn."

"So they do," said Selene as she looked at the top of my head. "You should pick some of the ends up at different angles and put ribbon or colored wool through. I've seen some girls do that and it looks great."

"I like mine neat," I said.

Selene looked sad again and sighed heavily. "Sorry. I guess I don't know much about hair and beauty. That's Nessa's realm."

We sat in silence again apart from her occasional sniffing. I searched my mind for something to say to make her feel better the way she had just made me feel when she said that I was pretty and cute.

"Erm… Selene, you know how the Moon orbits Earth?"

"Yes. Course I do, about once every twenty nine and a half days."

"Exactly and that's why we call a month a month! Moon equals month. How many of the other planets can say that they have words used about them? And not just any word. Not an obscure word. Month is a word we use all the time…" I said, as everything I'd ever read about the Moon in Dad's books came back to me. I'd learnt some of it off by heart for a school assembly. "To many early civilizations, the Moon's monthly cycle was an important tool for measuring the passage of time. The Hebrew, Muslim and Chinese calendars are *all* lunar calendars. In fact, the *New Moon* phase is uniquely recognized as the beginning of each calendar month just as it is the beginning of the Moon's monthly cycle."

Selene smiled and looked more cheerful. "You're a clever little thing aren't you?"

I felt more cheerful too. Most people's eyes glazed over with boredom when I told them about stuff that I'd read like that, but Selene looked like she was genuinely listening to me.

"And you're far from dull," I continued. "The Moon is one of my favourite planets because you don't just stay the same. You have all the different phases you go through. Erm, let me see if I can remember them. New, New Crescent, First Quarter, Waxing Gibbous, Full…"

"Waning Gibbous, Last Quarter, Old Crescent and back to New again," Selene added happily.

"See that's what makes you interesting. You could never be dull not with all that going on and words being named after you."

Suddenly she giggled. "'Month' isn't the only word named after me. Another word to do with the moon is 'lunar' and then 'lunatic' as in mad person. Loonie."

"Oh," I said. "Um. Well I am sure that makes you interesting too."

And then she began to laugh. "Looo-natic," she said drawing out the word. "That's me. Loonie petunie.

Lunar lunatic."

Her shoulders began to shake in a silent laugh. It was catching. Soon my shoulders started to shake too and the more she laughed, the more I laughed. She said, "Looonatic," again then I said it, "Lunatic. Maaa-aaad." It was like this wonderful private joke that just the two of us got and the more we said it, the funnier it seemed. Selene lay back, slid down the remainder of the stairs, and landed on the first-floor landing in a heap in hysterics. I slid down after her. We couldn't stop laughing. Pat, Nessa and Yasmin rushed out of my room to see what the noise was.

Pat took one look at us, shook her head in dismay and said, "lunatics," which of course set us off again and soon we were both lying on our backs, tears running down our cheeks while Pat looked on, wondering what she'd said.

Nessa shook her head and sighed. "She's always like this when the Moon is full."

Selene smiled up at her. "Ah but that's what makes me interesting. Right, Thebe?"

"Right, my loonie friend," I said and I put my hand up to high five her and she high fived me back. Selene then coughed and tried to make her face go straight. I did the same but then her shoulders started to shake again and that set me off too and we ended up laughing so much that I got cramps.

Chapter Six

Sunshine and music

<u>Thebe's list of things to do</u>
Text Hermie, again.
Do homework.
Do weekly internet shop. Order extra
juices for all the visitors we've had
lately. Check shampoo and bathroom
supplies.
  Check out exactly what is going on in
my horoscope and what those planet
people ought to be doing!

On Wednesday night, I got home to find *another* of the planet people was visiting. This time, it was Sonny Olympus or Mr O as Dad told me he liked to be called. "A big hunk," Mum said when she told me that he was in the living room. Her and Dad were certainly starstruck and so was I when I first set eyes of him. He was awesome. He was sitting on the sofa smoking a cigar and was very handsome in a white-teeth, chiselled-jaw, Hollywood-movie-star kind of way. He radiated fabdom.

He beamed a hundred-watt smile at me. "So you must be Thebe? Sun in Virgo?"

"Yes. That's right," I replied and began to splutter as the smoke from his cigar made my eyes water and my chest feel tight.

Mr O stubbed his cigar out immediately. "Filthy habit, sorry about that. So. I suppose you have the usual Virgo allergies: wheat, dairy, pollen and aversion to smoke?"

"Some," I said and I crossed the room to open the window.

"Too bad. So then, little lady. What can I do for you in your zodiac month?"

"Who me?" I blurted. I was surprised by his question as the other planet people who had been over this week appeared more interested in Mum and Dad than me (apart from Selene), and I was starting to accept the fact that my zodiac month was going to be a non-starter – the stuff you read about in books but doesn't happen in real life. I turned back to him after opening the windows. "Er, you could tell me where my guardian is. Hermie. He doesn't reply to anything and he gave me a special phone but he doesn't answer it."

"Not sure where he is, but before he left he asked me to pop over while he's gone incommunicado," said

Sonny with another bright smile. "Bummer to get Mercury retrograde when you're Zodiac Girl, but it happens sometimes. It's different for everyone and if that's in your planetary line up, then there's not a lot you can do."

I found myself warming to him. "Yes. I guess I was hoping for an exception seeing as I'm Zodiac Girl this month. I wondered if I'm supposed to be doing anything or if I've done something wrong?"

Sonny closed his eyes for a moment. "Okay. Now let's see if I can remember. I took a look at your chart before I came out. Uranus landed a surprise on you. He been over?"

"Uri, the Uranus man? Nope."

Mr O shrugged. "He does his own thing. The rebel of the zodiac as you probably know. He likes to do the opposite of what people expect, so I always expect the unexpected if you get my meaning. Now what else? Oh yes, Mars has been in opposition to the Sun in your first house. The job of Mars is to bring up troublesome issues in the home. You had troublesome issues here, kid?"

"Sort of. Erm, family stuff," I said with a glance over at Mum. I didn't want to say too much in front of her about how much I hated sharing with Yasmin in case she thought I was being mean. "Erm… room-mate."

"She's had to share with her cousin," Mum

interjected. "It's show down time between her parents, both Leos, neither will back down—"

"I can imagine," said Sonny.

"So Yasmin's come here for a short stay," Mum continued.

"Oh I get it. And Thebe, you like your room neat and you like your own space, huh?" asked Sonny.

I nodded. "Dad said that girls are often Zodiac Girls at turning points in their lives so I thought maybe that me having to share was my turning point. Like I'm supposed to learn something from it."

Mum looked at me proudly. "Thebe's a very bright girl," she said. "She catches on really fast. And she virtually runs this house single-handed. She took over when she was ten. Said she could do a better job than the rest of us and she has too. She keeps everything ship-shape and in order. She'll be running empires when she's older. You wait and see."

I did my best to smile modestly but Sonny didn't look impressed at all. "Hmm. So it looks like this aspect has been sent along to stir up some family stuff," he continued. "It will pass. Everything passes. And Jupiter is prominent at the full moon at the end of the month so that will be nice. But what's the root of this month? A difficult aspect to Saturn. There always seems to be difficult aspects to Saturn in all Zodiac Girls' charts."

"Dad said that too. He said that Saturn is the

taskmaster. The one who teaches you major lessons in life when he touches your chart. I wondered if it was to do with my cousin. I've been thinking about it a lot. I was really resistant when she got here and I'm still not happy about it but I reckoned that might be the problem. I have to let go and learn to share."

"Nope. That's not it," said Sonny.

"Why not?"

"It's never that simple with Saturn. You've just told me exactly what you need to do with that situation. You've worked it out, learnt your lesson and it sounds like you've given yourself good advice there. Nope, the lesson Saturn has to teach you is more subtle, deeper."

"So what is it? Dr Cronus was here the other day but he hardly even spoke to me. Can you help me?"

Sonny beamed again. "Maybe, maybe not. See, being Zodiac Girl, it's all how you run with it. You can't have expectations as it's different for everyone. Now then, how about you put on some music, we kick off our shoes and sit back and relax?"

Kick off my shoes? Relax. Was this man mad? I asked myself. It wasn't the time. I'd just got home from school and I had a list of things to do. "Can't. I got homework to do and—"

"You can do it later," said Mum, and she kicked off her shoes and looked coyly at Sonny.

He got up, took off his shoes too, pulled a CD from

his pocket and put it in the CD player. "Summer chill-out sounds. Just the thing for an evening like this when it's wet outside. I brought it specially. It's my favourite," he said. "Now let's draw the blinds, light us a candle Mrs Battye if you would, and let's all lie back and enjoy being in this wonderful room."

Our living room was the Scorpio-themed room. I called it the Goth room because it was painted blood-red with spooky paintings of dark angels and crows on the wall and huge silver candelabra in the fireplace, very dramatic. It wasn't my favourite room in the house partly because the paintings made me feel uncomfortable, but also because the heavy velvet curtains were a dust trap and they always set my allergy off when I cleaned in there. Mum got up and lit a candle in the fireplace.

"Okay, let's all lie on the floor," said Sonny.

"Can I be excused?" I asked. "I really do have stuff to do, a pile of homework and—"

"Thebe's an A star pupil," said Mum. "We never have to remind her to do her homework like we do our other daughter."

"Indeed," said Sonny. "Well even A-star pupils need some time off. What do you do to relax, kid?"

"Erm... play on the computer. I don't know. Crosswords sometimes. Word games. Chess. Surfing the internet. I like keeping busy. That's how I relax."

"Okaaaaay," said Sonny. "Yes. Good. It's good to work, excellent, but you've got to have balance. Light and dark. Yin and yang. Sweet and sour. So come on, kick back."

Mum made a face as if to tell me to do as I was told, so I took off my shoes and lay back on the floor.

"Hit the play button Estella, my friend," said Sonny and he lay down on the rug. "Ah, one, two, three, let's be in the moment and go with the music."

The swell of a hundred violins filled the air. I closed my eyes and began to listen.

I've never done anything like this before, I thought. *Just wait until I tell Rachel. Although I have listened to music but only when it's been on in the background. Oops, got an itchy foot.* I sat up and scratched my left foot then lay back down. *Wonder if Mum and Sonny have their eyes closed.* I couldn't resist so I took a peek. Yes, they both looked very peaceful. *Close my eyes. Okay. Come on, Thebe. Relax. Wonder how long it will take to do my French homework this evening? And I have to prepare for my history project too. And I suppose I'll have to have another go at ice-skating although I can't imagine I'll ever manage to do it. Oops, got an itch on my head.* I gave my forehead a scratch.

"Stop twitching, Thebe," said Mum. "She's such a fidget, Sonny. Can't ever sit still. Even when she's watching TV, her foot twitches."

"Just listen to the music," said Sonny in a dreamy

voice. "Let it wash over you."

My back hurt. It was hard down on the floor even if there was a rug underneath us. I made an effort to listen to the music though. It was quite nice. Soothing, but my mind was soon off again. It was mad. Like there was a whole pile of people in there commenting on what was happening and making lists of things to do. Lists? That's what I should be doing. Making my list of things to do. And they weren't the only lists I made. I had exercise books filled with lists. Lists of my favourite music, my favourite films. Lists of foods I liked and foods I didn't. My favourite people. Favourite books. Lists of my worries. My pet hates. My goals. I liked lists. They made me feel safe and secure. And I liked ticking off the jobs on the "things to do" ones. Tick. Tick. Tick. Done. There was always a nice feeling of having achieved something. That was how I relaxed. By writing lists and by getting things done, not by lying about in the dark.

"You're not listening to the music, Thebe," said Sonny. "Relax. Chill. Let it all go."

I made my mind go back to the music but I couldn't stay with it. My mind was too active. I liked Sonny but he wasn't much use. I opened my eyes and looked up at the dark ceiling.

Yasmin popped her head around the door, surveyed the scene and pulled a disapproving face. "Mad," she declared and shut the door.

For once I had to agree with her. Relaxation. Who'd have ever thought it was such blooming hard work?

Chapter Seven

Desperately seeking someone!

Another week went by and still no sign of Hermie. Not an email, not a call, not a text on my zodiac phone – which I checked regularly. My month as Zodiac Girl was almost half over and nothing had happened. Least not for me. Mum and Dad were having a merry old time entertaining their new planet pals, most of whom had been over while I was out at school. At least one of them was also over most evenings, hanging out, having beers and chatting in the study or sitting out in the garden by the pergola. It was looking lovely at the moment with tumbles of flowers cascading down over the trellis near there. It's usually my favourite time of year as all the roses, clematis and wisteria suddenly come into bloom, but this year I couldn't appreciate it. The Zodiac thing was bugging me. Not that anyone seemed that bothered about it except for me. Pat and Yasmin were happy as they appeared to have bonded with Nessa, who was often found in either my room or Pat's after school talking hair, make-up and nails while they listened to music. Even Selene, who I would have thought would have been more sensitive to my case, was over one night having a long conference call with Mum and Auntie Maggie and Uncle Norrece about how to fix their marriage. Seemed like the whole family was benefiting from being with the planets, apart from me. I had never felt so left out of anything in my whole life. I was starting to feel more and more wound up about it all to the point that I could hardly sleep, as my mind went over and over what I thought should or *could* have been happening.

One night after yet another pathetic attempt at ice-skating, I decided that I couldn't face going home again only to feel like the odd one out. Instead I decided to go into Osbury and see what the planets got up to when they weren't hanging out with my relatives at Zodiac Lodge. I particularly wanted to see if I could find Hermie.

I explained my plan to Rachel in the afternoon break at school on Friday, "If the mountain won't come to Mohammed, Mohammed must go to the mountain. You coming?"

"Wouldn't miss it. I love mountain climbing," she said, then when she saw my blank reaction added, "That was a joke, Thebe."

"Sorry," I said. "Course. Very funny. Sorry. Been a bit distracted lately."

"You can say that again."

"Been a bit distracted lately," I repeated to show that I hadn't totally lost my sense of humour.

Rachel rolled her eyes. "Okay. Just let me phone Mum and let her know I'll be late home," she said.

At least I have one friend in this world, I thought, as Rachel spoke to her mum. It wouldn't be a long journey – we had to get our school bus to the cross roads at the bottom of the hill then change onto the number seventy-three bus which would take us straight there. Easy-peasy. It would take about forty minutes.

"What do you do to relax?" I asked Rachel once we'd got onto the second bus after school.

"Watch telly," she replied. "Read. Sometimes I like to just lie on my bed and look up at the sky through the window and let my mind wander wherever it wants. Why do you ask?"

"No reason. Erm… do I strike you as a relaxed type of person?"

Rachel burst out laughing.

"Why is that funny?" I asked.

"Because you are one of life's doers, not one of life's dreamers. Knowing you, if you were going to relax, you'd have to make a list about how you were going to go about it first with a timetable saying when and for how long."

Not a bad idea, I thought, and I made a mental note to do just that. I could put relaxation on my list of things to do and include it in with my school schedule. I liked to highlight my different subject areas in different coloured markers. I enjoyed doing that almost as much as making my lists. I'd mark each subject in a different coloured felt pen. Green for geography, blue for history and so on. Yellow could be for relaxation. I had two separate sheets. One for the timetable at school and one for my homework schedule out of school. That way, I could see clearly exactly where I was up to and what needed to be done and what time was spare. Then I realized that Rachel was joking.

"I can relax. Really I can. Just everyone has their own way of doing it."

"Exactly," said Rachel, but she didn't look convinced.

We didn't talk about it any more because the bus had reached its last stop. We had arrived in Osbury.

Luckily for us, the rain that had been threatening earlier had blown away and the afternoon had brightened. We got off and surveyed the area. It was a pretty village typical of the South of England with a patch of grass in front of the bus shelter, a church at the end of the green, a bush of white roses by a hall next to the church and over the road a row of shops.

"Where to?" asked Rachel.

I pointed to the shops. "Let's start there first."

We made our way over the green and looked at the shops. There were the usual: chemists, newsagents, a charity shop, a hardware shop, mini-market.

"Doesn't look like the kind of place where planets would live," said Rachel.

I was about to agree with her when I spotted a deli. "Hah," I said. "Look over there. I bet that's the deli that Jupiter owns. Dad told me that's what he did. Look, it's called Europa and Europa is one of the four moons of Jupiter. Io, Europa, Ganymede and Callisto."

We went over for a closer look. It looked like any other deli. Tables, chairs, a counter at the back. A big notice on the door said CLOSED.

"Well, it is half past four," said Rachel.

"I guess. But most places don't close until six or so."

"Maybe he's on holiday. Hey," said Rachel when we walked on and she spotted a beauty salon. "Didn't you say that Nessa owned a beauty salon?"

I nodded. "And I bet that's it," I said when I noticed that it was called Pentangle. "That would be appropriate for Venus. A pentangle is a five-pointed star and that is often associated with Venus."

"Why?"

"I think that Venus makes a pentangle star shape as

it travels around the Sun," I replied. "Let's go in and see if anyone knows anything about Hermie."

We went up to the door but it was clear that no-one was there either. The blinds were down and on the door was a sign like the one at Europa. CLOSED.

"And I bet I know exactly where she is too," I said.

"Your house?"

I nodded. "Along with the others. Not to see me though. It was last week that my moon was conjunct with Venus. From what I've been able to see there are no encounters with her this week or next, but then I might be wrong. If only Hermie were here, he could explain properly." I pointed to another shop front towards the end of the row. "And there's the cyber café Dad talked about. It's also a magic shop."

"That's run by the Uranus planet man isn't it?"

"I guess so. At least it is when it's open," I said as I noticed another CLOSED sign. "What is it with this place? It's like a ghost town. Doesn't anyone work around here?"

Rachel pointed to a fish and chip shop. "That's bound to be open. Let's go in there. I'm starving."

"I wouldn't even bother checking," I said when I saw the name of the shop. Poseidon. "Poseidon's another name for Neptune. He'll be over having a beer with Dad." Right enough, when we got close enough to see, like the others, there was a CLOSED sign on the door. "Apparently some of them are at our house during the day too, having lunch, playing cards."

"You sound upset, Thebe," said Rachel and she linked her arm through mine. "Come on. I'll buy you some chocolate buttons to cheer you up."

I tried to smile but she was right. I was upset. I couldn't help it but I was getting more and more wound up about the fact that everyone in the world seemed to be having a good time in my zodiac month except me.

Rachel bought me the buttons and some crisps for her (I can't eat them as I am allergic to the MSG they put in them) then we walked up and down the street a couple of times and looked in all the windows. There was no sign of Hermie or any of the planet people. I even asked a couple of people in various shops if they'd seen Hermie or knew an office or building called Mercury Communications. Most people knew who he was but no-one could tell me where to find him.

"Gone on holiday, I think, love," said a young man with ginger hair in the chemists.

"Not seen him about lately," said an elderly Indian man in the newsagents. "He often disappears a couple of times a year. Goes off on that bike of his."

"I heard he likes to go to a spa resort," said an old lady in the charity shop. "One of those rest, get pampered, relax and recharge type places. Good for him, eh?"

After a good half hour, we had to catch the bus as Rachel had to be back home for her supper. I got on board feeling disappointed. We took seats at the back and as we sat down my zodiamobile bleeped that there was a message. My spirits rose in an instant as I glanced down.

"Merwanna peranna, oogie boogie blurh," read the message.

Rachel looked over my shoulders. "Is that planet speak?" she asked. "Do we need a dictionary to interpret it?"

I shook my head. "No. It's simply typical of the type of thing that can happen when Mercury is retrograde. Remember? Mercury retrograde means garbled messages? Miscommunications?"

Rachel cracked up laughing. "Brilliant," she said. "Because you can't get more garbled than that. Merwanna peranna, oogie boogie blurh."

I wished I could have laughed along with her but it didn't strike me as funny. It was just another disappointment in my "special" month.

Chapter Eight

Preparation!

"You making one of your lists?" asked Rachel when she found me sitting outside the hall just before assembly on the following Friday.

"Yep. Big night tonight," I said as I showed her my notebook.

<u>Thebe's list of things to do</u>

1) Hallway: Mars area. Remove shoes and coats not being used. Make sure there are flowers.

2) Living room: Pluto area. Needs dusting.

3) Study: Mercury area. Put books and magazines into neat piles.

4) Dining room: Jupiter area. Dust and polish. Shine glasses and cutlery.

5) Kitchen: Sun area. Clear and tidy all surfaces.

6) Mum and Dad's bedroom: Uranus area. Pick up all discarded clothes.

7) Bathroom: Neptune area: clean towels and new soaps.

8) My room: Venus area. Tidy my side.

9) Pat's room: ex-Moon area. No entry.

10) Spare room: Saturn area. Keep door firmly shut.

11) Confirm food and fruit punch.

"Long list. Big night? What's happening?" she asked.

"Mum's asked all the planet people over for dinner and I've decided that what I need to do is organize the lot of them," I said.

"Organize them? But why?" she asked as she looked over my list again.

"I think they're all spaced out. Seriously. Disorganized. They've forgotten what they're meant to be doing. I think they need a secretary or a PA or someone to do their schedules and sort them out."

Rachel looked doubtful. "I don't know. I mean, they're the planet people, you're the Zodiac Girl. Aren't they supposed to be telling you what to do?"

"That's just it. They're not telling me *anything*. I get home most nights to find one or two of them there lounging about in Dad's study or lolling in the garden – like, doing *nothing*. Anyone would think that they're on holiday. I told you about the other night when Sonny

83

was over. I mean lying about listening to music? Excuse me but what a waste of time that was. And Selene, although she's terribly nice. She needs to get a grip. Way too emotional. Crying one minute. Laughing the next. And Nessa, hanging out doing people's nails. I mean puhleese, has she forgotten who she is?"

Rachel still looked anxious. "I don't know, Thebe. It simply sounds to me like they feel at home at your place and who can blame them? It must be like their dream house."

"Maybe, but surely they have planet work to do?"

"Yeah, but even planet people deserve some time off, don't you think? And maybe how they choose to relax is their business, their choice. I mean, you can't control the planets, can you?"

"I'm not going to try and *control* them!"

"Well you know what you're like."

"What do you mean? What am I like?"

"Well you can be a bit… bossy sometimes."

"Me? Bossy? No way. Sit up straight, Rachel."

Rachel immediately sat up.

"That was a joke, Rachel."

"Oh! Course. But you do like to do things your way."

"I like to do things *right,* that's all. Like at home, if I didn't tell everyone what to do, we'd never eat or have clean clothes. And Mum and Dad love it that I colour co-ordinate their wardrobes. It makes it so easy for them to find what they're looking for. You should try it. All the dark colours together, all the whites in one place, all Dad's Hawaiian shirts together. It looks better too. So I run the household? That's not controlling. That's being *organized*. That's all. And this is supposed to my special month. I want to do it *right*."

Rachel shrugged her shoulders. "It's your call. So what are you going to do?"

"We'll have dinner, and then with them all there I'm hoping to make some plans—"

"And some lists," Rachel added.

I got the feeling that she was poking fun at me a little. She likes to do that sometimes when she thinks I'm going into what she calls one of my "I'm-going-to-take-over-the-world" phases.

"Yeah, lists. I want to synchronize dates in the calendar this month with those highlighted as important in my birth chart. I want to make sure that if any planet person has a part to play that they don't forget or ignore me. Like Saturn features strongly this month but he was over the other night and barely glanced my way. He was too busy with his nose in one of Dad's books. I also think that he wasn't very happy when he found out that the Saturn room was being used for storage – but at least he didn't cry about it like Selene did when she discovered that Pat had painted her out."

Rachel started laughing. "Poor planet people. Sounds like they're in for a telling off."

"No way. Just a... reminder."

Rachel squeezed my arm. "I'm only teasing, Thebe. And you're right. Some people do need organizing and you're *just* the person to do it! So tell me what you've got planned for the dinner?"

"The food bit's easy. Aunt Nikkya will cater as usual."

"Fab," said Rachel. "So what else?"

"I'm going to seat them at the same angles as they are in my chart."

"Angles in your chart? You know I don't understand astrology like you do. What do you mean?"

"In a birth chart, depending on where the planets are at the time of your birth, they sit at different angles to each other. Like they can be conjunct – that means within an eight-degree orb of each other, sextile – that means sixty degrees apart, square – that means ninety degrees apart, trine – that means one hundred and twenty degrees apart, opposite, which means one hundred and eighty degrees apart."

Rachel held up her palm and said in a robot-type flat voice. "Information overload, information overload. Brain's going to blow, brain's going to blow. What you're saying is that astrology is very complicated, yeah? Least it is to me. It's like you're talking Greek when you go on about trines and sextiles and stuff."

I laughed. "I guess. I wouldn't worry about it, Rach. It just means that I'm going to seat them in the right alignments."

"Can I come? I'll help you set up but you have to tell me what to do in plain English, not astrogobbledygook."

"Absolutely. I already asked Mum and she said you could."

Rachel clapped her hands. "Fab. Oh but, oh god, what if I can't remember who they all are."

"I've thought of that," I said and ripped a page out of my note pad. "Here. I did this for you. It's a list of who's who so that you can come prepared."

She took the list and glanced down it.

Sun: Sonny Olympus (or Mr O) actor. Big hunk.

Moon: Selene Luna. Counsellor.

Mars: Mario Ares. Ex-marine. Teaches self-defence.

Venus: Nessa. Runs a beauty salon and classes about how to find your inner goddess.

Pluto: PJ Vlasaova. Interior designer. Goth.

Uranus: Uri. Runs a magic shop and cyber café.

Neptune: Captain John Dory. Boatman and runs a fish and chip shop.

Mercury: Hermie. Motorbike messenger boy.

Saturn: Dr Cronus. Headmaster.

Jupiter. Joe Joeve. Deli owner.

"Thanks. That will help me remember," she said, "you really do think of everything."

"I try to," I said.

"What about the anti-stars? Yasmin and Pat?"

"As soon as they heard about it, they were both ringing around trying to find a mate's house to go to. I hope they do. In fact, I can't wait until Yasmin goes for good. It's been awful sharing with her. She treats me like I'm her least favourite person on the planet, which is so not fair. I did try in the beginning to make an effort to get on with her, but she hasn't tried at all."

Rachel sighed. "Teenagers can be difficult."

"*We're* teenagers, Rach," I said. "In case you hadn't noticed."

"You know what I mean. Older ones. They think they know everything. My policy is to pretend that they don't exist. So. Are all the planets coming?"

"Apart from Hermie. Seven o'clock is kick off. Be there or be square."

"Or conjunct or whatever," said Rachel.

I smacked her arm lightly. "Ha ha, very funny. Now shut up or I'll write you another list."

Preparations were already ongoing when I got home in plenty of time to help set out the table. Mum was up in her room buzzing with excitement and she had about eight outfits on the bed.

"I don't know what to wear," she sighed as she tried on a blue dress then turned to look at herself in the mirror. "Bit much? Does my bum look big in this?"

"No, you look great. All the outfits are lovely," I said as I got out my note pad and consulted one of my lists. "Erm... just checking that you know what to do tonight."

"Yes. Absolutely. Hand out the drinks, right?"

"Right."

"And you said you're going to make up a drinks menu for our guests to choose from."

"I've done it," I said. I'd spent the whole of the previous evening researching cocktail names on the Internet then adapting them for Aunt Nikkya's alcohol-free fruit punch. "Want to look?"

Mum took the list I handed her and glanced over it.

***Menu for the Stars ***

Jungle Jupiter

Saturn Surprise

Pluto Punch

Uranus Um Bongo

Venus Sunset

Mars Mojito

Moonbeam Margerita

Screaming Sun

Neptune Nightcap

"Fabulous, baby. You are a star," she said.

"No they are," I joked. "Rachel and I will be taking coats," I said.

"What time is Nikkya bringing the food and the punch?"

"Just before seven. All we have to do is pour the drinks then heat up the food up as usual. She's making ten varieties of her punch with a different fruit in each so that each planet can have their own."

"Excellent," said Mum. "I think they're going to like it. I checked and none of them drink alcohol so no need to provide any of that."

"Why don't they drink alcohol?" I asked.

"Mr O said they used to drink nectar of the gods and nothing compares to that, but then they haven't tasted Aunt Nikkya's fruit punch."

"They're going to love it. I do want tonight to be perfect, don't you?"

Mum nodded. "It will be."

"When will Dad be back?"

"Just in time. He's in the city doing a pre-recording for next week's show and meeting with that ice-skating lady. How are you getting on with your practice?"

"Oh, making progress," I lied. I didn't want to ruin the evening by telling her how useless I was at it.

Luckily she was far too involved with the

preparations for dinner. "Benjie said he'd heard back from everyone apart from—"

"Hermie," I finished for her.

She nodded. "And Mars and Pluto can't make it after all. Mario teaches a self-defence class he couldn't get out of and PJ, Pluto, had a house make-over to do, but don't worry hon, not many girls can say that they have a guest list like yours tonight, even if a few of them are missing."

I felt slightly miffed that they had come over and met Mum and Dad in the day while I was out, yet they couldn't rearrange things to get to our special dinner. I was determined that nothing was going to spoil our night. "I know. I'm not going to get upset about it. I think we're going to have such fun, even if a couple are missing."

"That's the attitude," said Mum.

Next door in my room, Yasmin was on the phone to one of her friends. "I am so out of here tonight," she said with no attempt to keep her voice down when I walked in. "My weirdo relatives have got an even weirder bunch of people over."

Good, I thought, *suits me*. I didn't want her around with her killjoy attitude. I went and tinkered on my computer while she finished her call. I wrote out the guest list then made neat borders around each of their names. After a while, I became aware that Yasmin was watching me over my shoulder.

"What are you doing?" she asked a few moments later.

"Place names," I said as I scrolled down so that she didn't see too much. I didn't want her poking fun.

She scrutinized the screen. "Neptune. Venus. Jupiter…" she read. "Are you having a fancy dress party?"

"Sort of," I said. I didn't want to get into who they really were with her in case she asked too many questions and then realized that my guardian had gone walkabout. She'd love to rub my face in that.

"Your family are bonkers," she said.

I smiled back. I could have said something about hers but bit my lip and agreed. "Yeah, I guess. Where are you going?"

"Sleepover with a mate. And Pat's coming too."

Yippee, I thought. *I get my room back for one night and maybe Nessa will pay me some attention too.* "Oh well, have a good time," I said.

Ten minutes later, we heard a car horn beep outside and then she and Pat were gone. I couldn't have planned it better. I focused on my computer and set about looking at images from the web of the various planets. My idea was to print out little place cards for all of them so that they'd know exactly where to sit. When I'd finished with the place names, I printed out my last minute "To Do" list:

Lay out outfit.

Bath and change.

Check food is all there.

Set table.

Set place mats according to my horoscope.

Light candles for atmosphere.

Have CDs ready, for atmosphere music.

Put the answering machine on so that there are no interruptions.

So there wouldn't be a full set of planets – at least the rest of the plan was going beautifully. This evening was going to be the best ever. I couldn't wait.

Chapter Nine
Star studded dinner

At seven o'clock, the doorbell rang and I went down to answer it. It was Rachel, right on time and she looked really pretty in a dusty pink top and rose pink skirt. She had also put in star-shaped silver earrings for the occasion.

"Perfect," I said.

"You look great too," she said. "Star child."

I gave her a twirl. I'd put on my best dress. I'd got it for Aunt Francelle's wedding last year. It was red with a halter neck and the material was covered in tiny silver stars. I also made sure I was wearing the pendant that Hermie had got me.

"So set me to work," said Rachel. "Where are we going to be?"

I showed her into the dining room. "In here."

"Jupiter room, right?" she asked. "I keep forgetting which is which. I could probably do with one of your lists to remind me."

"You won't need one. We won't go in any of the

rooms apart from in here and the kitchen. Jupiter is the planet of jollity and expansion so Dad thought that it seemed fitting that the dining room was done in his honour. Jupiter was also known in Roman times as the King of the Gods."

"Awesome. Has he been over yet?"

I nodded. "Earlier in the week. Not that he took much notice of me though."

"What's he like?"

"Big and jolly with a black moustache and very approachable for someone who's King of the Gods but then they're all playing it down. I guess they have to or else they'd attract too much attention."

"They have to go undercover, like cops on a job."

"Something like that. Remember, we saw Jupiter's deli in Osbury."

"Yes, Europa. Named after one of the four moons of Jupiter, you said."

"That's it. You're getting it," I replied as Rachel looked at the painting depicting Jupiter on the wall. It was another of Aunt Francelle's works and showed a majestic bearded man on a throne. In the background was a centaur – half man and half horse – which is the symbol for Sagittarius.

"Luckily the dining table is round," I said as I began to lay out the place names, "the same shape as a birth chart, so I can get people in just about the right positions as they were in the sky at the time of my birth."

"Right. Whatever," said Rachel as the phone in the hall rang and went onto answering mode. "Where shall I sit?"

"Over on the left, next to me. I'll put Mum, Dad, you and I over there – that should work as most of the planets in my chart are over on one side so I can put them all together. Except for the Sun, that's opposite to Saturn. See, there are a few houses in my chart that are empty. Dad said that's because I'm an old soul. He says you can always tell an old soul because they have all the planets piled in one place as if they have a last lesson to learn in one area of their life. I'm still not sure what that is for me. I was hoping to find out this month."

Rachel had a mystified expression on her face. "I have absolutely no idea what you're talking about," she said, "but I don't care. I'm just happy to be here."

I handed her some matches. "Fine. In that case, you just light some candles."

"That I can do," she said as the phone rang again. "Shall I get that?"

I shook my head. "I put the answering machine on. My zodiac phone is on in case Hermie or any of the planet people needs to get through."

The first guest to arrive was Dr Cronus.

"Drinks are in the Jupiter room," said Mum and directed him in to the dining room. She looked lovely and had settled for a smart, green silk trouser suit with a gold necklace and earrings. Dr Cronus looked like he'd also made an effort for the evening. He had on a smarter-than-usual tweed suit and waistcoat and he was wearing a red bow tie with tiny stars and planets on it. He bowed stiffly and followed Mum.

"He doesn't look like a barrel of laughs," whispered Rachel.

"He's not. He's a headmaster," I said.

"Eek," she said as we went into the kitchen to finish the drinks. They were all set out in their jugs and labelled so that I could see which one was which, and the room smelt wonderful with the scent of fruits and mixed spices.

Next to arrive were Nessa and Sonny. This time, she really did look like a goddess. She was wearing a white, off-the-shoulder dress and her hair was up with little diamante stars arranged through it. Mr O had a black suit and bow tie on as if he was going to a very posh dance.

Rachel's eyes almost popped out of her head. "They are the most glamorous people I have ever seen in my whole life," she whispered after we'd taken Nessa's wrap.

"Very Oscars," I agreed.

Selene arrived on her own. She too had dressed up and was wearing a silver silk top with a long shimmery green skirt. Around her neck, she had a moon pendant with matching earrings in her ears. "It's so generous of you to have this evening for us," she said to Mum. "We so rarely get the chance to get together like this."

"Our pleasure," said Mum and ushered her along the corridor to join the others.

"Is she the Moon lady?" asked Rachel.

Selene overheard and turned back to her. "I am, and I do believe you're Thebe's friend."

Rachel nodded. She seemed to have lost her tongue and had become shy, like someone meeting the Queen.

"This is Rachel," I said. "And her birth sign is Cancer."

"Which means that the Moon is your ruling planet," said Selene with an encouraging smile.

"Yes," whispered Rachel.

"Come on then," said Selene. "Let's you and me go and get to know each other. Us moonstruck types have to stick together."

Rachel glanced at me and I nodded. Okay, so it was someone else about to have a good time with one of the planet people in *my* month but I didn't mind it being Rachel. She was my best friend and I was glad to share some of the excitement with her.

"Please come through," I said. I could barely

contain my excitement and I knew that Mum and Rachel felt the same. As our guests began to fill the dining room, Mum caught my eye and then did a little jiggy dance on the spot as if to say she was having a great time.

By seven forty-five, Captain John and Joe had arrived and were in the dining room with the others. They were also in their best clothes and I stood at the door and marvelled at how sophisticated they all looked.

"So who's missing?" asked Mum.

I did a quick count round. "Hermie, no surprise there, Mario and PJ which we knew about, and Uranus."

"Uranus? Hmm," Mr O said. "He may turn up but you know what Uranus is like. The planet of the unexpected. He'll come in his own time, in his own way and it will probably be in some kind of extraordinary or eccentric fashion."

We decided to give Uri and Hermie a few more minutes while the others mingled and drank Aunt Nikkya's fruit punch. When each of them saw the names of the drinks on the menu that I'd put out, they seemed genuinely delighted.

I poured Mr O a large glass. "It's mainly juice," I said as he finished the glass in one gulp.

"Hmm, that's good."

"Would you like another?"

Mr O nodded and I refilled his glass then went around refilling the others and making sure everyone had what they wanted. It was always the same when we served Aunt Nikkya's punch. Everyone always loved it.

"You can tell that they feel comfortable here," said Rachel. After half an hour we refilled glasses, and took round nuts, olives and crisps again. She looked down at her empty jug of Neptune Nightcap. "We might need more of this one soon."

I nodded and followed her into the kitchen and looked on the counter where the jugs were. Most of them were almost empty apart from Hermie's.

"Everyone must be really thirsty," I said as I picked up a jug of Saturn Surprise to take into the dining room.

Dad came through with another empty jug. "Need a hand?" he asked.

"Drinks need refilling," I said. "They seem to really like it."

Dad winked. "They do indeed. It's that special Caribbean flavour that Nikkya creates. No one does it like her."

At that moment, Mum came through to join us and overheard him. "Do you know what her special ingredient is?"

I shook my head. "I can taste coconut and banana

but I'm not sure what else?"

"Spices, cinnamon, nutmeg," said Mum, "but apart from that, it's her secret."

"No worries," said Dad and he picked up a jug of Mars Mojita to take back into the guests. "It's a hit and that's all that matters."

We followed Mum back into the dining room and I glanced around. Everyone seemed happy, chatting away, laughing. Okay, so Captain John Dory's face looked slightly flushed and Dr Cronus's cheeks were almost beetroot and the noise level in the room had gone up a couple of decibels but that was a good sign that the evening was going well.

Just at that moment, the phone in the hall rang again.

"Get that will you, Thebe, baby," asked Mum. "It's been ringing all night – just in case it's Pat needing something."

I went into the hall and picked up. It was Aunt Nikkya. She sounded upset. "Oh thank god, Thebe. Have your guests arrived? What's happening there?"

"Yes, just about everyone's here. Why?"

"I've been trying all night to get through but no-one was picking up—"

"Is it something to do with the food?" I interrupted. "Something I have to do?"

"No. No. Just… okay Nikkya, take a breath," she told

herself. "Thebe, have you served the drinks yet?"

"Erm… some." At the other end, Aunt Nikkya let out a loud groan. "Oh *noooooooooooooo*."

"Why? What's wrong?"

"Honey. Oh god, oh lord, get them to drink some water or eat something or preferably go and lie down somewhere."

I felt a knot in my stomach twist tight. "What's wrong with the drinks?"

"Honey. It's in the punch. Your dad sent me over a message that your guests were allergic but… oh lord, it must have fallen behind the coffee and I only just found it on a post-it note. No honey. Oh lord, that punch is full of honey, it gives that special sweetness. Are your guests okay?"

"They seem to be," I said. "Listen, I'll call Dad out."

I dashed into the dining room and pulled Dad out into the hall and quickly filled him in on the situation. He said a few words to Aunt Nikkya then sat down heavily on the hall chair.

"But what does it mean Dad?" I asked.

"Oh Lord, baby girl, it's a disaster. I looked it up in one of my books after Hermie warned us that day when he first came over, which is why I sent the message over to Nikkya."

"Yes but don't forget with Mercury retrograde…"

Dad nodded. "Expect miscommunications, misunderstandings, messages to go astray. I should have known and double checked. Oh lord what are we to do?"

"But what will happen to them? Will they be ill? Will their faces blow up? How will it manifest?"

Dad sighed. "There is nothing more intoxicating for them. One drop and they'll be legless. Two drops and they'll be singing rugby songs. Three drops and... oh lord, oh my, you get the picture?"

"Think so. Um. I'd better go and warn Mum."

I raced into the dining room where I quickly filled Mum and Rachel in.

Mum glanced around. "I think that maybe we should serve food, get some solids in them and *quickly*," she whispered.

"Good idea," said Dad, "the effects are beginning to show."

I glanced around. They were all looking bright-eyed now. I picked up a fork from the table and tinged it on the side of one of the glasses. "Dinner will be served in a moment if you'd like to take your places," I announced.

"Wot already?" said Nessa. A few strands of her hair had come down and she was looking slightly cross-eyed. "No. Let's 'ave a dance first."

"Yes, let's dance," agreed Selene who was also

looking squiffy. "Put some music on someone."

"Yes, yes, music," said Dad and he went over to the CD player and read out all the titles he could with anything to do with the stars or the sky in them. "What do you fancy? Starlight Express? Moon River? Music from The Planets?"

Everyone started laughing hysterically as if he was the funniest comedian who ever lived. *It wasn't that funny*, I thought, as I watched tears roll down Joe's cheeks. Finally, Dad picked a disco CD and put it on. Within moments, they were all dancing away merrily. All with their own style: Selene doing a dreamy dance with swaying arms, Dad and Nessa started jiving, Dr Cronus put his arms around Mum and began waltzing, Joe did some Greek dancing and Captain John Dory attempted to do Irish riverdancing which made Rachel crack up laughing. When the second track started up, Nessa called out, "Make a line, let's do the 'okey Cokey. Let's do the conga."

Dad looked over, shrugged and held up his hands as if to say, *what can we do?*

"Great party this," said Mr O with a grin as they formed a line and off they went round the room, each one with their hands on the hips of the person in front.

"If you can't beat them, join them," said Mum.

"Just what I was thinking," said Dad. "Maybe it will be all right after all." And he and Mum joined the line.

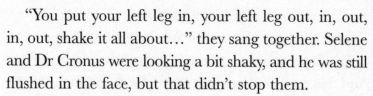

"You put your left leg in, your left leg out, in, out, in, out, shake it all about…" they sang together. Selene and Dr Cronus were looking a bit shaky, and he was still flushed in the face, but that didn't stop them.

"I think it's going to be okay," Rachel said with an anxious glance at them. "They're only dancing."

I told myself to relax. *Only dancing. Only dancing. Relax. Relax.* But my inner knot was getting more and more knotted as it twisted and turned inside of me. *Oops,* I thought, as I watched my esteemed guests and realized that they were behaving like a bunch of drunken relatives at a wedding.

Rachel turned to me and grinned when Nessa bumped into a cabinet and Mr O almost tripped over a chair. "There's nothing for it, Thebe, except to join them in the dance."

She ran over to the end of the line, put her hands on the last person who was Joe and off they all danced out into the hall and up the stairs. Unsure what to do, I ran after them.

"Come on, join in," called Rachel.

"Yes, come on, Thebe," urged Mum who seemed to have let go of any anxieties and was having the time of her life.

"Come on, Zodiac Girl," said Mr O.

And then with Nessa leading, they started singing. "Ole, ole, ole, ole, vum vum, vum vum. Ole, ole, ole,

ole, leg in, leg out, shake it all about…"

I tried to get Mum or Dad's attention. Dinner was ready. It needed to be served or else it would be burnt. And there was a thumping on the wall and the muffled sound of Mrs Janson next door yelling, "Keep that blooming noise down."

No-one took any notice as Nessa continued to lead the conga line. I stood on a chair and yelled at the top of my voice, "DINNER."

The line stopped and everyone turned to look at me.

"We *need* to eat," I said. "*Sit* at the table."

"Tee hee. Zodiac Girl hath spoken," said Joe. "We must obey."

"Yes, you must come and sit down. NOW!" I said.

Joe started giggling.

"And *you*, you're supposed to be King of the Gods," I said. "You should be setting an example, not acting like a lout."

Selene and Nessa cracked up laughing. "Jupiter. You're a lout," sniggered Selene.

He looked well put out and looked around at the others. Then his face cracked a huge smile. "This is like the parties we used to have on Mount Olympus in the old days. Remember? Ah, those were the days. Come on, let's do the Zorba dance." He summoned everyone into the position for Greek dancing – a line where they stood side to side with their arms along the shoulder of the person next to them.

"No, NO, time to eat. You need some food," I urged as I climbed down off the chair.

"We *need* to dance," said Selene and she looked as if she might burst into tears at any moment. "Nobody dances enough anymore. Come on, let's be butterflies." And she started flapping her arms like wings. *She really is loonie*, I thought as I watched her.

"That's true, need to dance," chorused Mum and Nessa and for a moment they looked sad, but then they began to be butterflies as well.

"Your mum is great," said Rachel and she began to be a butterfly too.

"Put on Zorba the Greek music," said Joe. "I'm King so I get to say what dance we do. In fact, no, forget the Zorba, let's do the plate-smashing dance. Mrs Battye, where are your plates?"

"NOOOOOOOOOOO," I said as a picture of a kitchen full of smashed crockery flashed through my mind. I climbed back up on the chair. "All of you BEHAVE. This is terrible. Have you forgotten who you are? No. You either do as I say or you leave now and NO SUPPER and *definitely* no pudding and Aunt Nikkya had made coconut ice-cream specially!"

The planet people and Mum and Dad hung their heads and looked at the floor like a bunch of naughty five year olds – but it had done the trick. They took their seats according to the table plan.

"She's very strict," Dr Cronus whispered to Joe as he wobbled past and sat down.

"I know," said Joe. "Scary."

Serving the food was simple enough and between Rachel, Mum and I, it was on the table in an instant. Everyone oohed and aahed and said it smelt wonderful. Aunt Nikkya was a great cook and, as everyone settled down to eat, albeit shakily on a few people's part, it appeared that the evening was back on course and was going to be a success after all.

"Welcome," said Dad. "Eat. Enjoy."

It was then that I noticed that Mr O was looking uncomfortable in his seat. He was scowling at Dr Cronus.

"Are you looking at me funny?" he asked.

"Maybe," the doctor replied.

"Well, don't," said Mr O. "In fact, don't look at me at all. It's very annoying."

"Not as annoying as you are sometimes," he returned. "Always wanting to be the centre of things."

"Hey guys, chill," said Selene.

"You can talk," Mr O replied to her.

"Me? What have I done? It's you that's full of yourself," said Selene.

"You can talk. No one's more full of themselves than you when you're full. The whole Earth gets to know about it!"

"So? Being full is part of what I do. I am the Moon you know."

"Now, now," Joe admonished. "Try and get along."

Selene, Dr Cronus and Mr O glowered at each other.

"Grrr," said Selene.

"Grrr," Mr O growled back and then he picked up a piece of bread from the bread basket and flicked it at her.

"Now stop it," said Joe with a glance at me. "In case Miss Strict Bottom starts up again because I, for one, want my supper."

"Miss Strict Bottom," sniggered Dr Cronus. "Tee hee. He said bottom."

"What's the matter with them?" I whispered to Nessa who was sitting next to me. "Why are they arguing and acting like five year olds?"

"Because of where they've been placed," she whispered back. "The Sun and Saturn are in direct opposition in your chart and now they are again, sittin' where they've been put by you. There are bound to be arguments. You've put Selene in at a strange angle too."

Oh no, I thought. Of course. It should have been obvious to me. The Sun and Saturn weren't the only ones in opposition. It wasn't long before Joe began to look agitated too.

"Don't like my seat," he whined.

"Me neither," said Captain John.

And they started on the bread basket too. First Joe flicked his bread at Selene. She flicked it back. Dr Cronus threw a chunk of his. It hit Joe on the head, so he joined in. Soon it was a bread fight with chunks of bread flying through the air and showering crumbs all over the place.

"Brilliant," said Mum. "These guys are such fun." And she *joined* in.

No, no, I thought. *This isn't how it's meant to go.* "Rachel, what should I do?"

"As your mum just said, if you can't beat them, join them," she said and *she* joined in.

The noise level was rising again, food was flying everywhere, everyone was laughing or yelling insults and I could hear Mrs Janson banging on the wall again.

"Les dance again," slurred Selene. "Les all be the sea." And she got up and started her funny sway dance. The others didn't take much encouragement to get up and join in.

Captain John looked particularly moved. "Yes. Let's be the sea," and he started waving his arms in the air.

Mr O went and put some music on, Nessa yelled, "*Conga,*" and off they went again, in a line, into the kitchen where Mr O found a laundry basket full of underwear. In a second, they all had a pair of Mum's big knickers on their heads. This caused great hilarity especially when Dr Cronus put on a pair that were pink with purple polka dots. Selene and Mr O were on the floor hooting with laughter and having hysterics.

"Stop it, *stop* it," I cried. "Put everything back in the basket."

But no one listened to me. Knickers on head, they got back in their line and conga-ed out the back, once around the garden and back into the hall.

"We don' get to let our 'air down very often," said Nessa as she danced past me, her hair completely loose and wild. "Come on, join in. Let's party."

I felt the knot in my stomach tighten so much I thought I was going to be sick. I felt my fists clench too. There was no way I could party feeling like this. I shut the door to the garden behind them and they conga-ed into the living room. "La la la la la la laaa,' they all sang.

And then I heard a scream. I ran to see what was going on.

"Cushion fight," said Captain John and whacked Selene around the head. She grabbed one herself and whacked him back.

"Come on," said Rachel who seemed to be having the time of her life. "I'm really good at this and so are you. Remember, you used to be pillow-fight champion."

"Yes, come on, Thebe," said Mum as her and Dad picked up cushions ready to join in.

I felt rooted to the spot. I couldn't believe my eyes. My honoured guests who had arrived only an hour earlier looking so sophisticated, had rolled their sleeves up and were playing and screaming like children. None of them heard the doorbell ring.

Hermie, I thought as I went to answer it, *at last, he's come to save the day.* I opened the door.

It wasn't Hermie.

"Now then, Miss. Are your parents or any adults at home?" asked a serious-looking, bald policeman with big teeth. "We've had some complaints."

Selene chose that moment to dance through into the hall. "Herro occifer," she slurred. "I'm re moon yunno. D'ya wanna a glass of Moon what is is? Majeecan. Mahittan. Moon milk. S'very nice. "Sgot honey in it. Not supposed to have honey, tee hee."

Dr Cronus came after her brandishing a cushion. "Gotya, gotya, you naughty little madam," he called as he waved the cushion in the air. Unfortunately, Selene ducked and the cushion bashed the policeman over the head. Gently, it must be said, but the officer was not amused.

"I think you'd better come with me, sir," he said.

Dr Cronus (who still had the knickers on his head)

smiled at the policeman and linked arms with him. "Where we going? Some'ere nice? And have you been a good boy today? Done your lessons? Good boy, you're very smart. 've you gorany honey? Hmm. Les be bees. Buzz buzz buzz just like a busy bee."

At that moment, the other planets emerged from the living room in their conga line again and as they did, I noticed Mum and Dad break off from the end and make a dive for the kitchen, closing the door behind them. Luckily, the policeman was so distracted by what was happening at the front of the house that he didn't notice them disappear.

"Ole, ole, ole, ole," sang the planets as they danced out the front door and down the path where four more policemen were waiting by a large van. One of the policemen opened the doors.

My last sight of our guests was as they were ushered into the back and taken off down to the police station leaving Rachel and I staring after them.

"Oops," said Rachel.

Chapter Ten

Paparazzi nightmare

The press went bonkers. It was in all the papers the next day. One of the broadsheets said:

"CELEBRITY ASTROLOGER, BENJAMIN BATTYE ENTERTAINS THE STARS

Arrests were made at the home of celebrity astrologer Benjamin Battye on Friday night, after complaints from the neighbours about noise. Eight disorderly people were arrested and kept over night in police cells. Staff said they'd never seen anything like it saying that the arrested party were 'off their heads', and 'behaving like lunatics'. One of them kept saying that she was the Moon and another claimed to be from the planet Venus, another said he was the King of the Gods, another the King of the Sea. The officer in charge said: 'I've had idiots in here before thinking that they were Napoleon or Cleopatra but this lot took the prize. Now I've seen it all.'"

Mr Battye and his wife, Estella declined to comment after their guests were taken away, but neighbour Mrs

Janson said that there had been "some very strange comings and goings" at the house in recent weeks.

The tabloids weren't as kind.

BENJY'S PALS ARE TRULY BATTY.

A fancy-dress party turned ugly when celebrity astrologer Benjamin Battye's guests went truly batty after drinking something named 'Aunt Nikkya's fruit punch', which was clearly a code name for something a lot more potent. All were carted off to prison after arguing with police officers and claiming to be from other planets. Selene (the Moon) Lune tried to kiss the officer in charge, Nessa (Venus) attempted to get Sergeant Watson and his colleagues to do the conga. Dr (Saturn) Cronus, an esteemed headmaster, hit a policeman then insisted on wearing a pair of bright pink knickers on his head and became hysterical if anyone tried to remove them.

"A right bunch of lunatics," said Sergeant Watson. "They should all be locked up for a very long time."

I had got out my Zodiamobile the minute after they'd all been carted off to the station and texted Hermie.

Urgent. All the planets except for Uri have been arrested. Please help.

But of course he hadn't replied.

"This isn't a joke anymore," I said to Mum the next morning after Dad had gone down to the police station with a big wad of cash to use as bail to get our planet friends out.

Mum was lying in bed with the curtains drawn even though it was ten o'clock. "Still no word from Hermie?" she asked.

"Not one. What's the point of having a guardian if he's not around when I need him? And I really need him now."

Mum winced. "Not so loud, baby. After that trouble last night, I hardly slept a wink and I've got a terrible headache."

"I'm not shouting," I replied. "In fact, I'm talking quietly."

"Well would you mind doing it next door, I need to sleep."

I tiptoed out. She did look tired and so had Dad this morning but he'd managed to drag himself out because a phone call had come from the police station saying that if he was willing to put up bail and vouch for them, then the planet people could be released.

In the meantime, Pat and Yasmin had come home after their sleepover. Both of them were absolutely livid. They had seen the morning papers and blamed me.

"You complete idiot, Thebe," said Pat as she

showed me the first paper. "*How* could you have let this happen? It will be all around school on Monday. How am I going to explain it? My street cred has been totally destroyed thanks, or rather, no thanks to you. You are the most stupid idiot on the planet. This whole family is stupid and now the whole world knows it."

"My sentiments exactly," said Yasmin. "I'm going to call my mum and dad immediately and ask them to get me out of this mad house as soon as possible. I don't want to stay here another minute in case what you've all got is catching!"

Well if Yasmin goes, at least some good might have come out of last night, I thought, as they flounced up to Pat's room and slammed the door behind them. I went to sit on the bottom stair. Outside, the sky was grey and it had begun to rain. *Just like how I feel,* I thought, as my eyes filled with tears. I really needed to talk to Rachel so I got up to get the portable phone and dialled her number.

"Thebe," she whispered when I'd got through. "I'm not allowed to speak to you. Mum's seen the papers and says you and your family are a bad influence. I will, of course, but can't just now."

In the background, I heard her mother. "Is that Thebe Battye? You put the phone down this instant."

"Later," I said. I didn't want to get her into any more trouble. Her mum had looked very angry when she'd come to pick her up and found the house surrounded by the police.

Just after I'd put the phone down, I heard a commotion outside. I went over to the window and looked out. Two people carriers had drawn up outside. Inside the carriers were six very grumpy and dishevelled looking zodiac people and Dad.

Minutes later, they trooped in, filed into the living room and slumped on the sofas and the floor.

"Thebe, fetch blankets and water. Lots of it. And strong coffee."

I nodded and set about doing what I was told. After they'd had their coffee, they settled down to sleep and soon the only sound was that of snoring.

"It's been a storm," said Dad as the doorbell rang, "but I think it will blow over. Get the door will you."

I went to the front and opened the door. A bright light flashed in my face.

"Any comment, darlin'?" asked a fat man with a pale face.

More lights flashed, almost blinding me.

"You Battye's girl?" asked a female voice.

"Were you 'ere last night?" asked a man.

"Any comment?" asked another man.

"Do you think you're from a planet then?" asked another, which caused everyone to snigger.

"We need to talk to the birds who say that they're

Venus and the Moon," insisted the fat man. "Exclusive interview with our paper."

"And we want that gorgeous geezer who says he's the Sun," said a lady with blonde hair and a lot of make-up. "Ask if he'll do a photo shoot in his boxers – espcially for the ladies."

"Phwoar, not 'alf," said another lady.

I blinked and tried to focus. There must have been about fifteen, maybe twenty of them.

"Daaaaaaaaaad," I called.

Dad came into the hall and got what was happening immediately. "Ohmygiddyaunt. Close the door, Thebe."

I closed the door and turned to Dad. "What's going on? Why are they all here?"

"Looks like they've sniffed out that there's more to the story, maybe even realized who they are."

"But people think that they're mad don't they, not that they're really from another planet? Surely it will blow over."

Dad shook his head. "I hope so, but it might blow our friends' cover while they're down here on earth. They might all lose their businesses and have to relocate. In the meantime, we have to protect them. This is bad. This could damage our reputation too. Everything we've worked for. No one will want to buy our merchandising and no one will want to read my columns. We'll be a laughing stock. The batty Battyes. Oh dear, Thebe. You have to go in there and wake them all up, explain the situation and let's see if we can get them out the back."

It wasn't an easy task waking six hungover planets.

"Go away," said Nessa. "I need my beauty sleep."

"Noisy, noisy," moaned Selene. "Be *quiet*, noisy person."

"Go and do your homework, child," groaned Dr Cronus.

"Hey! No need for that," I said. "I'm on your side. Look, there are more than a dozen paparazzi outside and they want to get in and photo you and interview you. Dad says they could blow your cover and destroy our reputation. What are you going to do?"

Dr Cronus sat up and rubbed his head. I was glad to see that he had taken the knickers off and, apart from bleary eyes, he looked back to his usual serious self. "Hmm. We have a crisis here. Now then, let's think. Okay, Thebe, do you think you've learnt your lesson yet?"

"Me! My lesson. What are you on about? It's you lot that have just spent the night in a police cell, not me."

"Your fault though," said Nessa, "you organized everything."

I was still reeling at what Dr Cronus had said and it seemed very unfair. I felt all the frustration I'd been holding back about being ignored in my special month bubbling up to the surface. "Listen here, you lot. Okay, so last night was a disaster but I did my best, truly I did. You're the adults. Tell me what to do."

Dr Cronus looked at me intently. "Hmm. We need Hermie really, don't we? Someone to talk to the press. That's his thing. Communication."

"I tried to call him but no reply."

"Retrograde," chorused all the planets who were beginning to sit up, rub their eyes, stretch and get up.

Dad appeared at the door. "Come on everyone," he said. "I've ordered the carriers to come back and wait around the back of the house. It's no problem. Thebe, what's happening out the front?"

I went over to the curtain and peeped out. A flash immediately blasted off. "Looks like they're still there."

"Right, off we go," Dad handed each of them a scarf as they traipsed past him. "Put these over your heads in case any of the photographers have slipped around the back. You know what a sneaky lot they can be."

Dr Cronus looked very put out. "This situation is very grave you know. I hope you all realize that this could be the end of our time here and that we may have to leave."

All the planets regarded me accusingly.

"Don't look at me. It's not my fault!"

Selene looked at me sadly. "Sometimes you have to

know when to stand up and take the blame."

"Come on now," said Dad. "No time to stand around. We need to get you out of here."

"My head hurts," groaned Mr O, who was looking extremely pale, even under his tan.

"Every bit of me aches," said Captain John Dory.

"Maybe we shouldn't have Zodiac Girls any more," said Dr Cronus. "More blooming trouble than they're worth, every one of them."

"At least you'll be remembered," said Mr O gloomily, "as the last Zodiac Girl ever."

"End of an era," said Nessa. "We need to go into hiding for a very long time."

They all trooped out the back like they had the weight of the world on their shoulders. I kept watch and then they were gone. *Maybe forever*, I thought.

Chapter Eleven

An unexpected visitor

I waited for half an hour then checked out the front again. The press were all still there leaning on the front wall, some of them smoking cigarettes. I opened the door and they all snapped to attention.

"You may as well go," I said, "because our guests have left."

"Where've they gone?" asked the fat man.

"Back to their planets probably," I said.

"Oh, she's a funny one," said the blonde as she strained to look over my shoulder into the hallway. "Come on lads, we'll track them down some other way."

One by one, they began to drift away. I closed the door and went into the kitchen where I plonked myself down at the table and put my head in my hands. *Nobody understands me or cares. I try so hard to do everything right and make life nice for people and now it's all gone and backfired.* I wished I'd never been chosen as Zodiac Girl and I wished I'd never met any of the planets. No good had come of it at all. I looked around the kitchen. The dishes hadn't been washed. Empty glasses were stacked by the sink. Uneaten food still sat in the pans. And I knew that the rest of the house was still a mess from last night – crumbs all over the dining room from the bread fight and cushions scattered in the living room from the pillow fight. Mrs Watson, the housekeeper, never came in on Saturdays, Mum was in bed and no way would Pat or Yasmin help tidy – it was up to me as usual. I began to make a mental list of what needed to be done. *I'll start in a minute,* I thought as I picked up a piece of bread from the table and flicked it onto the floor.

Cosmo crawled out of his basket by the door, hopped up onto my knee and nuzzled my nose as if to say that he understood. Tears dripped down my cheeks and splashed on the table, while outside the skies opened and rain began to pour. The kitchen lit up as a flash of lightning followed by the rumble of thunder sounded outside.

"Hi there, Cosmo," I said as I nuzzled him back. "I'm Zodiac Girl this month. Did you know that? It's a very special honour you know."

"Meow," he replied and put a paw up to my cheek. On hearing a noise in the garden, he suddenly leapt off my lap and ran to the window sill, hopped up, put his paws up and looked out.

"What is it?" I asked as I went and join him.

He seemed to be looking at something or someone intently. I soon spotted what. A tall slim man dressed in an electric-blue jump suit with silver spiky hair and a lightning fork painted on his face was standing on our washing line! He saw Cosmo and I staring and he waved and smiled, then began to walk along the washing line as if it were a tight rope.

"He's got to be Uranus," I said to Cosmo. His costume made perfect sense as both the colour electric blue and the lightning symbol were commonly associated with Uranus. I waved back at him but decided not to venture out. It was absolutely throwing it down. "I hope his gear is waterproof," I said to Cosmo as he began to move along the washing line.

It was like watching a circus performer. He walked the line, did a back flip which made both Cosmo and I gasp, then he got a small silver umbrella out of a pocket, put it up and skipped along to the end of the line. He hopped down onto the grass, went to a rucksack in the corner of the garden and hauled it on to his back. It looked heavy and he stooped under the weight of it. With bent knees, he did a wobbly comedy walk back over to the line, which he hopped back on to, then checked to see that I was still watching him. He stooped even more, grimaced and looked over at me as if for sympathy. Holding his back with one hand, and supporting the rucksack with the other, he began to walk across the line again.

"Wow! That must be difficult," I said. "Especially if whatever's in his bag weighs a lot."

"Meow," Cosmo agreed.

Every now and then, Uri checked to see that I was watching, nodded when he saw that I was, then he'd pull a parcel out of his rucksack and chuck it onto the grass. Then he went back to walking across the washing line. Then he'd chuck another parcel. Each time he let a package go, his back straightened up a little. I wasn't sure what to make of it. It was the strangest sight I had ever seen. It was still raining hard but he didn't seem bothered. As he reached the end of the line, he let a last parcel go and as he did, he straightened his back up completely so that once more he was upright and seemed as light as a feather. At the exact moment he tossed the last parcel aside, the sun came out from behind the clouds, lighting the drops of rain so they looked like thousands of tiny diamonds, and then he bowed. As he bowed, a rainbow appeared in the sky. It was magical.

I opened the back door and clapped.

"You must be Uri," I said.

He bowed again and skipped down off the line. "And you're Zodiac Girl."

I nodded. "I am but I'm trying to forget all that now. It's not been a very good time for me or any of your colleagues."

"I know. And I'm sorry I didn't make it yesterday to the party. It sounded like fun."

"You wouldn't be sorry if you knew what had gone on."

"But I do know. It was part of the plan."

"Plan? What plan? I mean… I had a plan but…"

"You're Zodiac Girl, yes?"

"Yes."

"So we all knew what needed to happen, more or less, in your month."

"No. That can't be. I mean, most of the planets took no notice of me…"

"That was part of the plan," said Uri and looked up at the sky. "Can I step inside? Bit wet out here."

Even though I knew who he was, I knew that Mum wouldn't want me to let a strange man into the house. "I have to check with Mum first. Wait here."

I ran up the stairs and into the bedroom. Mum was sitting at the window looking brighter than she had earlier.

"Mum, Uri's here and wants to come in for a moment. Is that okay?"

"I saw him in the garden. Marvellous show," she said. "Yes, let him in, but be sure to keep him away from the punch if there's any left."

"No worries. I poured the rest of it away," I said,

then I raced back down and let Uri in. Apart from his hair that was now plastered against his head and rivulets of rain that dripped down his forehead, he didn't look too soaked.

He stepped in and looked around the kitchen which was done out in the bright yellow and orange colours of the Sun. He bent down and stroked Cosmo who purred at once and then he sat at the table. His hair seemed to dry out in an instant. It spiked up all by itself.

"Uri, you don't seem to realize. What's been happening here, it can't be part of the plan. The other planets were all off their heads last night. Totally out of control."

"And isn't that life? Happens sometimes," said Uri with a shrug of his shoulders. "You can't control everything."

I didn't understand. He was making so light of it and it was really serious.

"No. It's all gone wrong. All of it."

Uri sighed. "Thebe, haven't you got it yet?"

"Got what?"

He pointed out of the window towards the washing line and the discarded parcels. "What we've all been trying to tell you?"

I felt myself go totally blank. "No. I guess I haven't."

Uri smiled. "To let go, Thebe. That's all. Let go. Sometimes things are out of your control. Sometimes you can control things, sometimes you can't. You have to recognize the difference. Sometimes you have to let go and go with the flow."

I thought back to his show in the rain and how he was letting go of the parcels and as he did, he became lighter. I looked around at the mess on the floor and on the table. And I thought about the past few weeks and all the odd things that had happened.

Suddenly I *did* get it.

I smiled at Uri, he smiled back, then got up, bowed and went out the door back into the garden and a second later, he had disappeared.

I looked around the kitchen and laughed. "Sometimes, you just have to let go," I said to Cosmo. I walked into the hall, into the study where as always, there were books and papers piled everywhere. "Lovely," I said. Next I went into the dining room which looked as if a bomb had hit it. "Marvellous," I said.

Finally, I went into the front room, scuffed aside some crumbs on the floor then lay out on the sofa. *I think I'll have a little snooze*, I thought. *So the house is a mess? So? No biggie. It's the weekend. Time to chill.*

In moments, I was in a lovely deep sleep.

Chapter Twelve

Chaos

Thebe's list of things to do
Chill.

"Mum, there's nothing to eat," moaned Pat as she looked in the fridge a few days later.

Cosmo looked down at his empty bowl then looked over at me. "Meow-ow," he said.

"Estella baby, this kitchen is in need of a good clean," said Dad pinching his nose. "It's beginning to smell." He lifted the lid on the bin. "Pooee! No wonder! This thing needs emptying."

Mum looked around in despair. "I know, the place is in a real mess. Let's have a cup of tea and decide what we're going to do." She looked hopefully over at me but I didn't budge.

"Good idea," I said. "I'd love a cup of tea. Thank you very much."

Mum sighed and went to the tea caddy. It was empty as I knew it would be. She sighed again and looked over at me with sad eyes.

Did I care? Not a bit. I was the new me. The chilled me. I was mastering the art of letting go. So far, I'd let go of making my bed in the morning, doing the groceries, cleaning up, making lists. Okay, so the house was a tip, but I was letting go of that too.

A gentle thud came from the hall announcing that the post had arrived. Dad went out to get it and came back moments later sifting through it. "One for you, Thebe," he said and chucked me a postcard.

It showed a white beach and a turquoise sea. I glanced at the sender. "It's from Hermie."

Dad nodded. "That would be right. The retrograde period for Mercury is over the day after tomorrow so I guessed that he'd be back in contact some time soon."

"What does it say?" asked Mum.

I read: Hello Thebe,

Hope you've been having a groovy time as Zodiac Girl. Back soon, will be in touch soon.

Love Hermie. PS: Been hanging out with your uncle Norrece over here.

Yet *another* of my relatives who had been hanging out with one of the planet people! I wasn't going to let it bother me though. So my guardian had spent the large part of my zodiac month on a Greek island. Cool. So he hadn't bothered to try and contact me until now, so what? He was going with the flow and now, so was I. It wasn't up to me to tell him what he should or shouldn't be doing. Nor anyone else for that matter. From now on, I was going to mind my own business and not ever try and organize anyone else's life again.

"Where's the card from?" asked Mum.

I looked at the postmark and stamp. "Greece."

"Of course, that's where Norrece was," said Mum.

"Greece! So that's where Mercury goes when he goes retrograde," said Dad. "I'd always wondered."

"And that's nice he's been hanging with Norrece," said Mum. "He'll be back soon. He and Maggie are getting back together thanks to the talks they've been having with Selene."

I should have done the same as Hermie, I should have followed his example and just relaxed these past weeks instead of getting myself into a frenzy, I thought, as I put my feet up on the table. "So. What's everyone doing today?" I asked.

"Well, clearly getting things organized around here," said Mum stiffly. "What time's the housekeeper coming? It is her day, isn't it?"

I shrugged. "Dunno. Has anyone contacted her?"

Dad, Mum and Pat shook their heads.

I glanced at my watch. "She probably came earlier

this morning as always but… did anyone leave the keys in the usual place for her?"

"What's the usual place?" asked Dad.

"I didn't know that there was a usual place," said Mum.

"Oh there is. It's under the Japanese pot on the shed porch, round the back for future reference. I usually leave it out for her when I bring the milk in on my way out to school but as it's half term this week, I haven't been out yet. Talking of the milk, has anyone remembered to bring it in this morning?"

"Look, Thebe, you've made your point," said Pat. "You ran the household. Fine. But you loved doing it. You know you did. You loved being in control and organizing us all."

"I know. But I've changed. I've realized that I have to let go. Let go of being a control freak. So that's what I'm doing. Letting go of running all your lives."

"But why, munchkin?" asked Dad. "You were so good at it."

"Ah but the planet people showed me that I was trying to control things too much and actually, it's okay if things get out of hand. It's not the end of the world if things go crazy."

"I'm not sure about that any more," said Mum as she looked at the pile of unwashed dishes in the sink.

"You have to go with the flow, Mum, and it will all

work out just fine. Trust me. Like the other night when our guests got arrested, I thought it was the end and when the press came the next day, I wanted to die. I thought I'd ruined it for Zodiac Girls for the rest of eternity – but hey, things worked out, the press moved on to another story and lost interest in us. The planet people are fine with it, in fact, according to Uri, it was all part of their master plan for my month as Zodiac Girl to teach me a lesson. And my lesson was to let go. So yeah, hey, let's go with the flow."

Pat, Mum, Dad and Cosmo looked at me unhappily.

I got up, found some cat food at the back of the cupboard and put it out for Cosmo. I couldn't let him be neglected in any way.

The others were still standing around as if they didn't know what to do with themselves. Finally Mum sighed, "Okay. Pat, you start on the dishes, Benjamin, you can clean the bathroom and I'll call Mrs Watson and see if she'll come out again. In the meantime, Thebe, do you think that you could do the internet shop? Get us some groceries in?"

"Maybe later if I'm not too tired. For now, I'm going to go and listen to some music."

I got up and went up to my room where Yasmin was lying on her bed with her headphones on. She barely registered my appearance. Like the rest of the house, the room was a mess, the bed unmade, clothes and socks on the floor. Instinctively, I went to pick up a pair of socks and put them in the laundry basket but I stopped myself. *Leave it, let go,* I told myself. *Stop being a control freak.* I lay back on the bed and chuckled to myself. It was all so clear to me now. I hadn't been ignored or abandoned by the planets. From the beginning, they had been trying to tell me to relax. Selene by trying to get me to let my feelings out, Nessa by demonstrating what it was like to have some girlie fun, Mr O with his chill out CD – all of them had been trying to show me how to chill by coming around and hanging out with Dad. I put the CD that Mr O had left on his visit into the player, put my headphones on and lay back on my bed to listen. It was nice music but I felt myself getting fidgety and my mind kept doing lists despite my trying not to. *Old habits die hard,* I told myself. I lay there for another five minutes. Part of me was itching to get up and tidy my room. It was like a force inside of me and I was having a hard time keeping it down. In the end, I couldn't stay there any more. I knew that if I did, I'd have to give in and tidy the room. I went downstairs to see how Mum and Dad were getting on.

"Hi baby," said Mum as she found a pair of Marigold gloves under the sink and put them on.

"Did you have a nice rest?" asked Dad as he put on

the Homer Simpson apron that was hanging on the back door and started to empty the bin.

Pat looked at me sulkily as she swept the floor, then she flounced out and clomped up the stairs.

"I hope you don't think I'm being selfish not helping out, it's just that I am trying to make the most of my zodiac month and for the first three weeks, I didn't get that they were trying to tell me that I have to let go."

"Baby," said Mum. "We only want what makes you happy. Really we do. And if you want to chill, then you chill, girl."

"Amen to that," said Dad. "Hey, Estella, let's boogie while we work."

Mum's face lit up. "Put on some salsa," she said.

I sat at the table while Dad put a CD into the player and then they got stuck into cleaning up, dancing and bumping bums along to the music. I wanted to join in so much. I wanted to put on the Marigolds and get stuck in with them. Nothing made me feel happier than seeing a gleaming counter surface in the kitchen or smell the lemon-clean scent of a freshly washed floor, especially when it had been very dirty. I found it so satisfying to make things better. Before my eyes, Mum and Dad were transforming the kitchen back to its usual pristine appearance. *I could start on the living room*, I thought, and almost got up to go and get the vacuum out from the hall cupboard. I pushed down the urge and sat on my hands.

I was chilling. I was letting go. Wasn't I? I went back to watching Mum and Dad cleaning and polishing. Dad began brushing the floor and dancing with the broom. He missed a bit of dust under the table. A feeling of frustration began to rise up from deep within me. I tried to push it back but it kept coming.

"Arrrrggghhhhhhhhhh."

Mum and Dad stopped what they were doing and turned to stare at me.

'What is it, baby?" asked Mum. "Somethin' bite you?"

"No. *No*. It's hopeless. *I* am hopeless." I got up and stood in front of them as if they were a jury and a criminal. "My name is Thebe Battye and I am a control freak. I can't help it. It's who I am. I've tried to fight it. I really have but I am beyond help, even the help of the stars. And I am sorry but I have to give in to it." I hung my head. "It's bigger than me. It's bigger than all of us." I took the brush from Dad and began brushing under the table. "See Dad, you missed a bit. You weren't doing it *properly!*"

Chapter Thirteen

Yasmin

"I guess you'll be going soon?" I asked Yasmin when I found her upstairs later, still lying on her bed. For once, the room was quiet and she didn't even have her headphones on.

She nodded but she didn't look happy. "Mum's flying back tomorrow so I'll be going home."

"You okay?" I asked.

"Like you care," she replied.

I went over and sat on the end of her bed. "It will be nice to have my room back. I'm not going to lie but you're still my cousin and I do care."

Yasmin's eyes filled up with tears which she quickly brushed away.

"What's the matter?"

"N... n... nothing," she said but her eyes were still shining with tears, which she once again attempted to brush away. "J...just... waghhhhhhhhhhh."

I let her cry for a few moments but I felt so awkward not doing anything. I tentatively put my hand out and found hers. I was half expecting her to shove it away but she didn't. She held it fast and then she sat up, wrapped her arms around me and sobbed into my shoulder.

"Ohmigod. What's the matter, Yasmin?"

She sobbed for a few more minutes then sniffed, reached out for a tissue and blew her nose. "Sorry," she said.

"But I'd have thought you were happy that your mum and dad had got back together," I said.

"I am. I really am but… just… well…"

"What?"

"Oh everything's wrong in my life."

"In your life? How? Like what?"

"I'm going to miss being here."

"I thought you hated it and thought that we were all mad."

"Not really. I like it here. I love that all the rooms are done up in different colours and different styles. I like that your dad dresses like a beach surfer. My dad is so straight and our house is cream. And beige. And boring."

"Oh but it's so tidy." (Aunt Maggie was a control freak like me and kept the house spick and span).

"I know that but it's like living in a hotel, nothing out

of place."

"But won't it be good to be home?"

"In one way but… I love that people are coming and going all the time here and… you never know what's going to happen next."

I was amazed at what she was saying. "I didn't know. I…"

"No one knows the real me," she said. "I'm really good at keeping my feelings to myself apart from today because I feel… well… I feel rubbish."

"You can always come and stay."

"No I can't. There's not room and I know you haven't liked sharing with me. You made that very clear and I don't blame you either. I wouldn't want to share my room with me."

"I haven't minded that much Yasmin," I said and I attempted a smile. "It's got easier."

"How?"

"I realized I had some things to learn."

"You? Like what?"

"Like I don't know everything and I don't have to try to be perfect and I have to chill."

"But that's what's awesome about you. You are so perfect."

"Me? No way. I'm the black sheep of this family. The odd one out."

"No. It's *me* who's the odd one out. Like your whole

family are so colourful and interesting. I feel so drab compared to you. Miss Ordinary."

"No. That's *me*. I'm not colourful or interesting."

"Yes, you are. You're amazing. You do everything so well and are so organized. I so wish I could be like that."

I couldn't believe what I was hearing. This wasn't the Yasmin that I knew. "Yasmin, are you on drugs?"

"Course not."

"But I thought you hated me."

"No. Never hated. I envied you and your naturally sunny nature. It made me want to rub you out because you showed me up for being such a Miss Misery. Like you're so thoughtful – you left me oranges and flowers and in return I was mean and spiteful."

"I thought you hadn't even noticed."

"I did. And I'm sorry I didn't say. I was *so* angry when I got here.

So mad with my mum and dad for falling out and not even considering how it affected me.

It was me who got turfed out of my room and my home. No one asked what I wanted. I was mad with them and I took it out on you, but it wasn't your fault and I… I am sorry."

"I think I took it out on you too," I said and I gave her another hug and laughed.

She pushed me away. "Why are you laughing at

me?"

"I'm not laughing at you. Just… we're more alike than we realized and here we are competing for the title of the dullest member of the family. It's… quite funny if you think about it."

Yasmin regarded me for a moment and then her face split into a grin. "I suppose it is, but it's definitely me. I get the prize."

"No, I *do*," I said. "I'm the black sheep."

"No, it's me," said Yasmin but she was smiling.

"Tell you what," I said. "We can be black sheep together."

Yasmin held her hand out. "Deal."

"Deal."

I should have known, I thought as we shook hands. *There was me on my side of the room with all my stuff and there was her on her side and both of us pushing the other away when we could have been getting on instead.* "And I'm sorry we wasted so much time not getting along. We could have had a nice time together." And then I had the most *brilliant* idea.

While Mum, Dad and Pat got to grips with the rest of the house, Yasmin and I attacked the spare room. We threw out a pile of junk onto the front lawn ready to be taken down to the charity shop, took all the merchandise that Mum wanted to keep and stacked it in the garage, then we got to work cleaning. I was happy again as I dusted and hoovered and polished with Yasmin at my side. When the room was sparkling, we moved the spare bed in and a few of Yasmin's belongings that she didn't need to take home with her. The Saturn room was only a small room but we made it look cosy and welcoming with some of Mum's posters and zodiac merchandise. Dr Cronus would be happy with it if he ever made it up the stairs and Yasmin was absolutely delighted.

"Voila," I said. "One spare room that is yours whenever you want to come and stay, because you are and always will be very welcome here."

"Thanks, cuz," said Yasmin and flopped onto the bed with a satisfied sigh.

Chapter Fourteen

Hermie's return

"Here he comes," said Dad as we heard the roar of a motorbike in the distance on the Saturday morning.

Mum, Dad and I went and stood in the front garden. Mum put an arm around my shoulder and gave me a squeeze. "Now remember, Hermie's about communication so you make sure you have a good talk to him and tell him all you've been going through."

I nodded. "I'll try." I wasn't sure I could explain to anyone the turmoil that had been going on in my head in the last few days. I wasn't sure who I was any more. How I was supposed to behave. My feelings were all mixed up and nothing seemed to help. My zodiamobile had started ringing the exact date that Mercury began to go direct and all the various planet people had been in touch. Suddenly they all had a lot to say as if they were making up for the first three weeks.

Trust in your dreams, Captain John Dory had texted. Hah! I thought when I'd read that. My dreams were more like nightmares lately. I'd be cleaning and cleaning a floor but it remained dirty.

Selene had called to tell me to trust my feelings. Double hah! My feelings were all over the place. One minute I was happy doing my usual thing: making lists, organizing my life, then I'd feel guilty because I was supposed to be letting go. So I'd try and let go and be chilled and not succeed, and *then* I'd feel bad about that. So, trust my feelings? How could I when they were so confused?

Mars sent a note saying: make goals, Thebe, that's the thing. Pff. I used to have clear goals and knew exactly where I was going, but now I didn't know what to aim for – to be chilled or to be sorted. Like with the ice-skating thing – should I let it go and admit that I was a failure? Or should I have another attempt at it and succeed by letting go on the ice? It was so confusing.

Enjoy your life, Mr O said. *Easy for him to say*, I thought. *Being the Sun, he brightens up everyone's life by simply showing up.*

Just make sure you do your lessons and hand your homework in on time, said Dr Cronus in an email. But hadn't trying to be the best at everything been what got me into such a mix-up?

Eat, drink, be merry, said Joe, the Jupiter man when he popped round one night to see Dad. I tried my best to do that. I ate, I drank, but being merry seemed to have escaped me for the time being. I'd never felt so wound up.

Venus also came over one evening and braided my hair into a funky new style with red wool threaded through. "At least you can look chilled, even if you're not feeling it," she said, and my new style did look cool. At least she didn't try to tell me what to feel or how to be.

Uri sent me a rubber fish and a bag of potatoes. No note. Dad said that was typical of him as he is the eccentric of the group. "One thing you can always expect from Uranus is the unexpected," he said. I put the rubber fish in the sink and wondered if there was some secret message in Uri's gift, just as there had been when he walked the washing line throwing off parcels. If there was, I couldn't fathom it.

I was hoping that Hermie was going to make sense of it all. His motorbike slowed down and he jumped off, took off his helmet and shook out his hair. He looked tanned and handsome, every inch the Greek god, and I could see that Mrs Janson was peeking out from behind her curtains. I turned, gave her a wave and she darted back out of sight.

"Presents from abroad," said Hermie and he reached into the box on the back of his bike. He handed Dad a bottle of something called Ouzo, he gave

Mum a tiny statue of a Greek god and a bracelet made of shells to give to Pat later. I waited for my turn and hoped that I wasn't going to be forgotten again. I needn't have worried, he pulled out what looked like two shoes boxes. "This is for Thebe, my Zodiac Girl," he said.

"What are they?"

"A surprise," he said. "One is for me, one for you."

I opened my parcel to find that it was indeed a shoebox but inside there weren't shoes, there was a pair of beautiful white ice skates. I gave them straight back. "No," I said. "I can't skate, and as part of my letting go of trying to be the best at everything, I am admitting it here, in public."

Hermie looked disappointed that I didn't want his gift.

"But what about that party?" asked Dad. "You're still going to come to that, aren't you?"

"I might come and just watch," I said, but even as I said it, I knew that if I went and all the others were skating and I wasn't, I was going to go straight back to feeling like the boring one of the Battye family.

Hermie regarded me closely. "Come with me and I'll look after you."

"Yes. Why don't you go, baby?" Mum said, "and Dad and I will come and join you."

"I could give you a ride on my bike," said Hermie.

"I have a spare helmet."

"I can't," I said. "I can't skate and I've never been on the back of a bike."

"You just hold on and let go," said Hermie.

"That's contradictory. How can you hold on and let go at the same time?"

"One's physical, the other's mental. Give it a try."

I didn't want to appear ungrateful or difficult. "Okay," I said, "I'll come on the bike, but I'm not skating."

He gave me a helmet which I put on, then Mum and Dad helped me up behind him onto the bike. "Hold on, let go," said Dad then laughed.

It was all right for him, I thought, *he'd be coming in a nice safe car.*

Hermie started up the bike, and va-voom, we were off, whizzing down the street. I clung onto Hermie's waist and shut my eyes tight. Air whooshed past making a roar in my ears. After a few minutes, I dared to look to my left. Our neighbouring houses were a blur of terracotta and I felt as if I'd left my stomach back at the house. I shut my eyes again.

"You okay back there?" asked Hermie.

"Errfff," I called back and clung on even tighter. *Okay, I'm doing the holding on bit,* I thought, *that seems to be going all right, now I need to do the letting go bit.* "Let go, let go, let go," I whispered to myself. I opened my eyes again. I stared at Hermie's back, I didn't dare look around in case I threw up. I decided to shut my eyes again. *One thing at a time*, I told myself. I could hold on, but letting go was still an alien concept.

Ten minutes or so later, we slowed down and stopped. I hopped off and Hermie took the bike to the car park area while I waited for him on the steps and tried to stop shaking. Mum and Dad weren't far behind, they parked alongside the bike and got out the car with a cheery wave.

Once inside the foyer of the rink, Mum and Dad went to hire skates from the cloakroom for her and Dad, while I went with Hermie into the skating rink. It was empty.

"Where are all the skaters?" I asked.

"They'll be here this afternoon," said Hermie. "We've got exclusive hire of the place for the rest of this morning. My gift to you for having had a rough first three weeks of your zodiac month."

"I'm still not skating," I said. "I… I'm not being difficult. I just can't." The thought of it terrified me.

"We'll take it a step at a time," Hermie said, and he slipped his trainers off, sat down and put on his skates. "Watch me first."

In a flash, he was up and on the ice. He was wonderful to watch as he moved with the grace of a dancer and the speed of an athlete.

"Almost as if he had winged feet," said Dad, as he came up behind me.

"Well, he would, wouldn't he? Being Mercury," said Mum coming to join us.

Mum, Dad and I watched in awe as he sped around the ice, span around, skated on one foot, the other held aloft, skipped, leapt, then held positions as if he was a statue. After a display worthy of the best professional skater ever, he came back over to where I was and pointed at the skates. "Ready to give it a shot?"

I laughed, or rather snorted. "I don't think so."

"Just give it a try," said Mum. "We'll all hold each other up."

Dad nodded encouragingly.

The three of them stood and looked at me with pleading eyes.

Mum started doing a silly dance, walking back onto the rink and beckoning me with her arms. "Thebe, Thebe Battye," she said in a daft dreamy voice that I supposed was meant to sound like she was trying to hypnotize me or put me into a trance. "Come on to the ice, come on to the ice."

Dad took his cue from her and joined in, doing the same beckon and silly voice. "Come on to the ice."

"Okay. Okay. If only to get you to be quiet and stop being so embarrassing." I gave in and sat down to put the skates on. "But I'm not going far."

Dad gave me the thumbs up. "That's my girl."

When I had the skates on, Dad and Hermie helped me to my feet and I walked to the rink like I had bricks on my feet. "Don't let go," I begged.

"We won't," Dad promised.

As soon as we got onto the rink, I let go of Hermie and grabbed the surrounding wall with my left hand. I hadn't even tried to skate but already my feet felt clumsy and my knees were giving way.

"Now can you see?" I asked. "I am not going to be able to do this. I've tried, I really have and I can't."

Hermie stood by my left side. "Give me your hand," he said.

I shook my head. "Can't."

"We've got you," said Dad. "You can let go."

I shook my head again. In the meantime, Mum had skated off into the middle of the rink. She lacked the grace that Hermie had and wobbled as she skated but she was staying up. As she was wearing a pink tracksuit, she resembled a blancmange and I couldn't help but smile.

Dad giggled too. "If your mother can do it, you can," he said.

I took a deep breath and gave Hermie my hand again and between Dad and he, they pulled me out into the middle of the ice.

"I don't like it," I said as we began to move across. "I don't want to do it." I wanted to go home to something familiar and do something I knew I was good at.

"Couple of circuits," said Hermie, "then if you really want to, we're out of here."

I felt a knot in my stomach as they pulled me along between them. On the second circle of the rink, I began to feel that I could trust them and relaxed a little.

"That's it," called Mum. "See, baby, you can do it."

And then my knees buckled and I lost my balance which caused Dad to wobble and then, like dominos, we all went over. One, two, three, onto our backs.

"Ooch," I cried as my bottom hit the ice.

Hermie was up in a flash and offered me a hand up.

"Argh," groaned Dad. "You okay, munchkin?"

To my surprise, I was. I'd fallen. I'd survived. I looked at my hands. No one had skated over my fingers.

At that moment, music blasted out from the speakers that were positioned on the ceiling. Great disco music with a good beat, the lights went up and soon after, Mr O appeared at the gateway to the rink. He was looking very dapper in a white tracksuit with a silver stripe up the side. He skated out onto the rink and like Hermie, was a natural. He skated around once then did an amazing circular jump.

"Ah yes, the half loop," said Hermie as he watched him. "Full rotation jump with a loop entry, and – yes! – landing on the back inside edge of the opposite foot. Marvellous." He clapped, Mr O bowed, then Hermie leant over to me. "He's such a show off isn't he? Thinks he's the centre of the universe."

I laughed. "Technically, I guess he is, being the Sun and that," I said, but I knew what Hermie meant.

He skated over to join us and he and Hermie helped me and Dad up onto our feet and together, I had another go around the rink with Mr O on one side, Hermie on the other. This time, we didn't fall over and for a few moments, with the music blasting, I felt as if I was flying. *Totally cosmic*, I thought, when for a moment I glanced to either side of me and realized who was supporting me. Skating along with the Sun and Mercury isn't your average Saturday morning. Once round again and the sensation got stronger. And then I realized that Mr O had let go and gone off to join Mum and Dad and it was only Hermie who had one of my hands.

"No! Argh!" I cried as I panicked, lost my balance and fell backwards again. Thewhump. "Ouch."

Mum and Dad were over again in an instant. "You okay? You had enough?"

I knelt up, rubbed my backside and decided that I was okay. And I wanted another go. This time, Mum and Hermie took me around. After a while, I started to sense that I had my balance. I could feel it, I just had to get my weight distributed right. "You can let go, Mum but keep hold of me, Hermie, please."

Mum let go and skated off and Hermie and I whizzed off on our own. "You're doing really well," he said as he slowed the pace down a little. "I was told that you catch on to things fast and you're doing fantastic. Now strike out to the left, that's it, now the right. Keep the balance. You're doing just fine."

Now that I had him to myself for a few moments, I decided to take the opportunity to tell him what I'd been going through. "I haven't felt fine lately," I said. "In fact, I've never felt so mixed up, like I don't know who I am any more."

"Who really does?" said Hermie, as he led us for a break by the wall. We stood, caught our breath and watched the others who seemed to be having a good time in the centre. "Finding out who you are is a lifetime's lesson. You're changing and growing all the time. Finding out who you are is an ever-evolving process."

I thought about that for a moment. "I guess. But what I was trying to say is that I don't know what I was supposed to get from this month. I don't know what I was supposed to do as zodiac girl."

Hermie nodded. "Actually you didn't or don't have

to do anything. It's all taken care of, but it can be tough when your guardian isn't around to explain things – but as Uri said to you, me being away was all part of the plan. It was no coincidence that your zodiac month fell when I was on my hols, I mean, ahem… retrograde. Nothing could have been more perfect for you at this time for what you need to experience."

"*Perfect?* But it was a mad plan."

Hermie chuckled. "Nope. It's all unfolding exactly as it should. See, sometimes it's not what life chucks at you that makes your life, it's how you react to it."

"What? Like if life throws lemons, make lemonade?" I asked quoting one of Aunt Francelle's favourite sayings.

"Something like that. You always have a choice, be miserable or make the most of things."

"But isn't that what I was doing in my own way, making the best of things? Organizing my mad family, doing my lists. I knew where I was with them."

Hermie nodded. "The upside of being a Virgo is that you can be tremendously well-organized and efficient. The downside is, you can be—"

"Controlling and obsessive," I finished for him.

He grinned. "Yep."

I remembered what Mum had said about Hermie being communication, so I decided to tell him my worst fears. "And there's something else…"

"What's that?"

"I… I was worried that the reason none of the planet people, and even you, weren't interested in me is because I am so boring. The black sheep of the Battye family. The rest of them are so glam and interesting."

"Thebe," said Hermie. "You are interesting too. Don't you know that? Your chart says that you have the potential to do great things. Haven't you ever wondered about why you're so good at organizing?"

"I just do what comes naturally. It's nothing special."

"Believe me, Thebe, it is. You have what it takes to be a very high achiever. Already, you're an A-star pupil – but this is the worry for people like you. You can burn out. You work, work, work, that's why if you can get what we're trying to tell you in this month, your zodiac month, you'll be set up for a lifetime. To be the best, you have to find balance in your life. Understand that and you will go to the top and stay there."

"You really think so?"

"It's all there in your chart. You're a top girl," he said, then he laughed. "You just have to watch out that you don't burn out or let your batteries go flat. Now. Want to see me go retrograde?" He began to back away.

"Noooo," I called but he was gone, skating backwards. He did a lap of the ice rink in reverse, then returned. "Now, want to see me go forward?" And off he went, skating ahead as normal. I watched and laughed. After another lap, he came back. "Ready to try on your own?"

What he'd said to me had made me feel so good that I felt that I could take on the world. I was a top girl. Possibly a high achiever. Not boring. I nodded. "But hang onto me until I'm ready," I said.

Hand in hand, we skated out onto the ice. The music was still blasting out.

"I think I can do it," I told him after we'd skated for a few minutes.

"Sure?"

I nodded.

"Find your balance," he said.

I smiled back at him. "I'll try."

He let go, and off I skated, on my own. *Balance and let go*, I thought as I sailed off. *Balance and let go.* It felt wonderful. Flying along to the music I began to think about which foot went where and what my arms should be doing. Immediately, my knees wobbled and down I went. Once again, Mum and Dad skated over, their faces full of concern.

"I'm okay," I said. "And I can do it! Almost."

They helped me to my feet and together we skated

to the wall.

Mr O and Hermie were skating together and once again, I marvelled at their grace.

"You have a good chat with Hermie?" asked Mum.

"I did, and I think that I understand what they've been trying to tell me," I said.

"What's that, munchkin?" asked Dad.

"I can be who I am. I can be me, Thebe, who likes to be in control, just I have to know when to let go. Hold on, let go, and it's all about balance."

"Sounds like good advice." Mum smiled back.

I felt the knot that had been in my stomach for the last few weeks begin to unravel and I felt lighter. It was going to be okay. Mercury going retrograde hadn't been the disaster that I'd imagined and my zodiac month hadn't been a waste of time. I'd got it. It had taken some time, but I'd got there in the end.

Hermie looked over at me from the centre of the rink and beckoned me over. I gave him the thumbs up. I could do it. It was all a question of balance. And if I lost it. So what? I could always get up and try again. Things didn't have to be perfect all the time. And neither did I.

I pushed off from the wall and skated towards him.

A week later it was the night of Janet Johnson the celebrity ice-skater's party. Load of press were there and

Dad had invited all our family. Auntie Francelle, Aunt Nikkya, Auntie Maggie and Uncle Norrece (who were all loved up again), Yasmin, Pat, Rachel and Hermie. At first there was a freestyle skate off for everyone and I felt so relieved to be able to join in and not be the only one from our group out on the benches watching.

About an hour into the evening, Janet did a solo performance and it was breathtaking to watch her as she appeared to fly on the ice. She really was the business, almost as good as Hermie and Mr O, but not quite. The audience loved her and cheered and cheered, then she went off to have her photo taken for the papers.

After that, various guests got up and did turns while we watched, and it was soon after that that Hermie came up behind me. "Your turn," he said. "Ready."

I gulped then nodded. "Ready."

"She wants to see all of you Battye family skate," he said and I looked over to see that Mum, Dad and Pat had their skates on and were beckoning me onto the ice.

I can do this, I thought as a wave of panic flooded through me. *I can do this*. Hermie had given us some practice sessions over the week and shown us a simple routine that looked good but wasn't too challenging. I stood up, put my skates back on and went to join them.

"Nervous?" asked Dad.

I nodded and he took my hand and squeezed it. "Me too, but we'll help each other."

Mum gave me an encouraging smile and the four of us held hands and skated out into the centre of the rink.

"And now for Benjamin Battye, celebrity astrologer and his family," said a man at a microphone by the side of the rink.

A spotlight beamed onto us, music with a disco beat started up and we went into our routine. Shimmy, shake and skate. It was only four minutes, round the rink, a little rotation, part reverse then we bowed. The rink erupted in applause and I looked around at the guests watching us and felt a warm glow of happiness. I felt like a star. For once, I was there with Mum, Dad and Pat, *me*, Thebe Battye, at the centre of attention along with them, not standing in the shadows watching as one of them took centre stage. Yasmin was grinning and waving and I spotted Hermie next to her in the benches. He nodded and gave me the thumbs up. I gave him the thumbs up back and promptly fell on my bottom.

The Virgo Files

Characteristics, Facts and Fun

August 24 – September 23

Patient, kind and well-organized, Virgos are wonderful listeners and calm in a crisis, making them the perfect sign to have as a close friend. They are often shy but don't be fooled – Virgos can stand up for themselves if they need to!

Don't invite a Virgo to your house if you have an untidy bedroom – they are often obsessively tidy and can't stand mess. These guys want to look perfect and can be materialistic. They like to have the best clothes, but they are unlikely to lend you anything in case you ruin it!

Element: Earth
Colour: Blue
Birthstone: Sapphire
Animal: Cat
Lucky day: Wednesday
Planet: Ruled by Mercury

A Virgo's best friends are likely to be:
Taurus
Capricorn
Cancer

A Virgo's enemies are likely to be:
Aries
Leo
Libra

A Virgo's idea of heaven would be:
A nice long walk in the country followed by a healthy meal.

A Virgo would go mad if:
They had to spend time in a pigsty!

Celebrity Virgos

August 25   ✳   **Rachel Bilson**

August 26   ✳   **Macaulay Culkin**

August 28   ✳   **Shania Twain**

August 29   ✳   **Michael Jackson**

August 30   ✳   **Cameron Diaz**

August 31   ✳   **Van Morrison**

September 2   ✳   **Keanu Reeves**

September 3   ✳   **Charlie Sheen**

September 4   ✳   **Beyoncé Knowles**

September 9   ✳   **Adam Sandler**

September 10   ✳   **Ryan Phillippe**

September 15	✳	**Tommy Lee Jones**
September 18	✳	**Jada Pinkett Smith**
September 19	✳	**Jeremy Irons**
September 20	✳	**Sophia Loren**
September 21	✳	**Nicole Richie**
September 22	✳	**Scott Baio**

Thebe's Gorgeous DIY Wall Organizer

You will need:

Thick card, about 30 cm x 50 cm

Some drawing pins (in a colour of your choice)

Some quilt padding (you can buy this in craft and fabric shops)

Some cool fabric – big enough to cover the cardboard

Several metres of thin ribbon

Method:

Cut the padding so that it is 10 cm wider and longer than the cardboard. Cut your fabric to the same size.

Wrap the cardboard with the padding and then the fabric, and pin them at the back with the drawing pins. Place your ribbons in a criss-cross pattern over the board, and pin them where they cross one another.

There you have it! You can slip notes and reminders under the ribbons, and you'll never forget anything again!

Are you a typical Virgo?

It's the beginning of a new term. What do you do the night before your first day back?

A) Pick out an amazing outfit. Start as you mean to go on!

B) Make sure all your books and folders are organized and your bag is packed – that way you can keep on top of all your homework.

C) Make sure you've read all the textbooks and know exactly what your timetable is so you're prepared for anything!

A bedroom says loads about your personality. What's yours like?

A) A mess. There are clothes everywhere, and you can never find anything.

B) Organized chaos. You know exactly which precarious pile your homework is in . . .

C) A place for everything, and everything in its place. You can't sleep in a messy room – you'd have nightmares!

Where are you usually hanging out at a party?

A) On the dance floor, showing off!

B) Having a chat with a close friend – you're a bit shy with strangers but you love hanging out with your mates.

C) At home! You hate parties – you'd rather stay in with a good book.

You're packing to go on holiday. What's your strategy?

A) Leave it until the last minute, and then chuck stuff in. If the suitcase won't close, sit on it!

B) Pack light – just a few items that all match each other. That way there'll be more room in your bag for souvenirs!

C) Make a list a week before you leave of all the things you might need, and check things off as you pack them. You'll be prepared for anything!

It's the end of term show. All the parts are up for grabs. Which of the following describes your attitude?

A) Move over Cameron Diaz, there's a new star in town. You are going to go for the lead and get it. You love to be the centre of attention.

B) Me, act? You have to be joking; I hate people looking at me.

C) You'd like a part in the chorus as you are a great team player.

It's your birthday next month and you fancy having a party. What's your plan?

A) Invite people on the day – no one would turn down the chance to come to one of your parties!

B) You'll have a think about music and stuff, but you don't need to plan the details until nearer the time.

C) Start sending out invites now, and make a detailed itinerary for the day. That way nothing can go wrong!.

How did you score?

Mostly As – vaguely Virgo
You try, but those Virgo organizational skills escape you!

Mostly Bs – versatile Virgo
You've got lots of Virgo patience and generosity, but sometimes your untidiness gets the better of you . . .

Mostly Cs – very Virgo
Neat, tidy and organized, your Virgo personality will take you far. Remember to relax sometimes though!

A selected list of titles available from Macmillan Children's Books

The prices shown below are correct at the time of going to press. However, Macmillan Publishers reserves the right to show new retail prices on covers, which may differ from those previously advertised.

All Pan Macmillan titles can be ordered from our website, www.panmacmillan.com, or from your local bookshop and are also available by post from:

Bookpost, PO Box 29, Douglas, Isle of Man IM99 1BQ
Credit cards accepted. For details:
Telephone: 01624 677237
Fax: 01624 670 923
Email: bookshop@enterprise.net
www.bookpost.co.uk

Free postage and packing in the United Kingdom